D1414990

BABY
SONIAT

BABY SONIAT

A Tale
From The Jazz Jungle

By
Neal Holland Duncan

St. Lukes Press
Memphis

St. Lukes Press

Distributed by Peachtree Publishers, Ltd.
494 Armour Circle, N.E.
Atlanta, Georgia 30324

Library of Congress Cataloging-in-Publication Data
Duncan, Neal Holland, 1944-
  Baby Soniat : a tale from the jazz jungle / by Neal
Holland Duncan.
     p. cm.
  ISBN 0-918518-75-X : $16.95
  I. Title.
  PS3554.U4644B3   1989
  813'.54—dc20   89-8748
                                                         CIP

For information address:
St. Lukes Press
4210 B.F. Goodrich Boulevard
Memphis,Tennessee 38118

ACKNOWLEDGMENTS

First and foremost I owe an unpayable debt of gratitude to Glenn Truitt. Without his interest and supreme effort in the preparation of this manuscript, this book would have remained embryonic.

FOR
BABY SONIAT
WITH A
FIREFLY AND LANTERN
LOVE, STILL

But when youth, the
   dream, departs,
      It takes something
   from our hearts,
      And it never comes again.

   Something beautiful is vanished,
      And we sigh for it in vain;
   We behold it everywhere,
      On the earth, and in the air,
   But it never comes again!

   "The Flight of Youth"
   ——*Richard H. Stoddard*
      (1825–1903)

BABY
SONIAT

1

Baby Soniat, molasses-voiced

Delta beauty, legendary debutante, and cross-country heartbreaker became old today at Saint Peter's Cemetery on Valence Street, and so did I. To her mother she had always been the most worthless white child ever birthed. To "all those others" she had been the loved, the envied, the lost.

Baby and I pre-date today's mongrel age. We go way back. Back to the days when white-teethed, long-limbed, sun-kissed, white Anglo-Saxon youths were not becoming refugees in their own country.

To me, like Baby now another fraying child of pride and privilege, she has been everything and ultimately nothing. Each born to play. Each paying the price of pursuing eternal youth.

Stebo Soniat, her father, had named her "Baby." Actually, Stebo had named her "My Baby," which is not really so unusual when one considers the fact that Stebo's real name was Steamboat.

Stebo's father, Judge Ravenal Soniat's, two great passions had been steamboats and hangings. The Judge, however, was catholically ecumenical. He hanged everybody: rich and poor, black and white.

Stebo had three great passions: Baby, drinking, and fornicating. The only time Stebo wasn't drinking was when he was winning a big case in court. If it wasn't big, Stebo wasn't interested. It was the same with his women. Unlike many who are libidinous-minded, Stebo actually fulfilled his desires with all the discrimination of an amorous rabbit. I always wondered why he had married Miss Fanny. If Miss Fanny had ever been big, she had long ago shrunk.

She was invisible even in her own drawing-room. Mother once commented on the long and interesting silence they had shared at a bazaar sale, and made certain they never worked the same booth again at Trinity Episcopal, New Orleans' church of the celestial snooze for Uptown society, on Jackson Avenue. Mother's ilk were perpetual moneyraisers. (Today's liberals are quick to shout that a Mississippi River of cheap labor perpetuated such social consciousness.)

Anyway, Miss Fanny became very visible, as well as vocal, after Stebo's death. Stebo's stallion-heart had literally burst from pride at the Boston Club the afternoon he heard the news that Baby was to be Queen of the Mystick Krewe of Comus, the most eminent and oldest of the Mardi Gras balls. (I mean, even the Duke and Duchess of Windsor bowed and curtsied to "Comus Royalty" when they were in New Orleans in the 1950's!) The year before, Baby had been Queen of Carnival. This made Baby the first-ever "Double Queen," and the tribute to her unprecedented.

On Mardi Gras night, when the giant doors that separate the two balls open at Municipal Auditorium, it is Rex and his Queen who walk over and bow to Comus and his Queen as the orchestras play "If Ever I Cease To Love," the memory-stirring song which is Mardi Gras' theme:

> *If ever I cease to love,*
> *If ever I cease to love,*
> *May the fish get legs*
> *And the cows lay eggs*
> *If ever I cease to love!*

Mardi Gras is really two celebrations. For the "Throw Me Something, Mister," it is the greatest and biggest free show on earth. For those belonging to krewes, the men's organizations that dominate the lives of the city's inner circle with their great balls and courts, it is a carapace of manners with its own system of royal inheritance where traditions are carefully preserved. That's why, in the social hierarchy built around Carnival, it is men rather than women who dominate society; and that, in itself, is a uniquely New Orleans experience.

While our families may not have instilled aggressiveness in us, that sense of knowing who we were and being socially different never escaped any of us. Baby's method of setting an example, however, was not as traditional as mine. She believed that if we could no longer lead America, we could at least teach it how to play.

And God how we played. The magnificent frivolity! Unquiet souls led by Stebo Soniat's small queen. Above all, we enjoyed one another. We brought exuberance and wit to all we did, from the endless childhood flirtations at the Clubhouse to the complicated love affairs of adulthood at the country club.

The Clubhouse had been built in the Twenties as a children's country club and was a miniature of its adult counterpart, except it didn't have a golf course. Just two blocks off the Avenue on General Pershing, it was our special sphere from the age of twelve to graduation from Country Day. The Clubhouse was our training ground for the adult world, right down to the engraved brass plaque secured to the back of the door of the men's lavatory that read: "Young gentlemen are requested to adjust themselves and their clothing prior to leaving."

When the Clubhouse closed this year, a bankrupt club in a bankrupt city, its special place in my heart closed and died forever, too. It was here, the night of the Beauty Ball, that Baby, Queen of Beauty, willingly let me drag her to the darkened lounge where we exchanged a first-passion kiss that ended with her pushing me away to ask, "What's that hard thing pressing against me?"

4

In the ballroom there was a stage for pageants and, at the foot of this stage, a jukebox that required no coins. Hugging the walls of the room were about eighteen banquettes. The largest banquette was in the corner and accommodated three tables. From here, safely ensconced, we reigned, knowing all the unwritten rules that defined membership to our exclusive encampment. Many were called but few were chosen. Baby was the social magnet, of course. The cynosure.

Mary Fern Bird, who has hated Baby since our first day at Country Day, once asked Baby, "Why do you think you can always get away with anything?"

"Because I'm truly beautiful. That's why, Mary Fern," Baby sweetly smiled. "I also don't have those awful crinkles across the bridge of my nose that make you look like a bunny rabbit sniffing clover."

Poor Mary Fern Bird, she hasn't spoken to Baby since. How many years has that been? Why, that's been over twenty-five years! But Baby didn't lie. Mary Fern did, and still does, resemble a bunny rabbit. Not that anyone had noticed until Baby called attention to the fact.

With Baby it's always high summer for us exiles from silver frames. I think this because my favorite photograph of Baby was in a large silver frame. The picture was taken in the Royal Enclosure at Ascot. Baby is leaning against a chocolate-mousse-colored Bentley, wearing a bias-cut silk flowered dress and wide-brimmed straw hat adorned with a rose that's the color of

5

her pink oval lips. The double-looped Soniat pearls stretch nearly to her waist. In the foreground, a linen-covered table has been laid for tea, and champagne is chilling in a silver cooler. It was her most famous photograph. Its message is clear: Poverty sucks.

Anyway, if Stebo wasn't turning up at the children's garden to stare at Baby adoringly, my grandfather, Boland Ferdinand Ball, was turning up to glare at everyone but me. (Ferdinand had been the name of his grandfather's prize stud bull.) A mountain of integrity, Boland Ferdinand Ball had been dubbed "Senator" at birth by his mammy because he was born "looking just like one" right down to his lifelong and very dignified paunch. It was over this paunch that the Senator swagged a heavy gold chain with a gold pocket watch at one end and at the other end, a gold locket containing a lock of his mother's hair, and a belle-ish picture of his wife, my grandmother, Eva Elizabeth. In the middle of this thick chain, above the unbuttoned last button of his vest, hung an ornate fob. Some said he was also born wearing his pince-nez. He was never without them. In fact, he was buried wearing them.

The Senator firmly believed the sinking of the Titanic had been a symbol of the approaching fate of Western Civilization. He owned that genius flowers in bad soils, but breeding will win out. "Breeding talks, breeding is not counterfeited. Remember that, Sudduth." Those were his last words to me on the day he died at home in the hospital bed I still have.

The Senator also didn't sanction the "med-dlesomeness" of preschool authority. "A child has too little time to be free," he'd say, but really he just wanted me with him all the time. He glared because Country Day staff referred to him as a "disruptive influence," a disruptive influence which resulted in my being expelled twice with impunity. The third time was for good.

Even then, Baby craved excitement and she'd be so excited when either Stebo or the Senator appeared at Country Day that her shell-like ears would turn pink.

"I wish my daddy would get me expelled. You're a lucky devil, Suddie."

Her wish came true the day Stebo arrived roaring drunk to take her to celebrate his hav-ing won another big case.

I lost my heart to Baby at the Broadwater Beach Hotel in Biloxi, Mississippi. Uptown people had places at the coast then. Some still do. Houses damp with dignity and help. Where sil-ver was still polished every Wednesday. The loca-tion of residence might change, but civilization prevailed.

Papa and I had gone to pick up a Connecti-cut couple he and Mother had become semi-friendly with at the Greenbrier the year before. We had the 1939 yellow, wood-paneled, Ford station wagon then that Papa loved so. He called Mother and the wagon his proud beauties. Some-times she was jealous. (I was very thankful Papa

7

was dead years later when hurricane Audrey came through like the big bad wolf and blew the wagon and the cottage away.)

It hadn't taken death to canonize Papa. Life had already done that. Instead he died in Japan at the age of forty-two and ended up having three funerals, the third because his body was lost for four weeks between San Francisco and New Orleans.

It's a heavy burden being the son of blindingly handsome parents. Raiford Garland Spencer: idealistic, gregarious, perpetually good-natured. Arabella Louise Ball: spirited, innocent, isolated. Romance surrounded them. They eloped after knowing each other forty-eight hours, and my grandparents refused to receive them or acknowledge their existence until I was born nineteen months later.

Even people who knew them would stare as if seeing them for the first time. Their being so casually oblivious to this attention only enhanced their personae. In retrospect, they were too intelligent to be totally oblivious. Let's just say they were kind about it. When Landry Pope and I were in "King Periman's Wish," their late arrival stopped the play until they were seated. That was when Landry and I were in Lower School at Country Day. Even then she was a three-erection beauty.

Good Lord, I haven't thought of Landry in a hundred years. We were voted King and Queen of May Day in 1951 and 1952, a double honor that would not take place again, and were husband and wife in "Mr. & Mrs. Good English."

Landry had a breakdown during her parents' unquiet divorce and started putting out in Middle School. When Tweet Green whispered to me that Landry had been caught "doing it" with Geoff Badel on the playing field, I told him he was a damn liar and asked him to remove his glasses. Then I knocked him down. Landry was a thoroughbred, though. Lord knows she was. The next day she was back at school. Before class, I walked over and asked her if it were true.

"Yes, Suddie, it's true," she answered, looking me squarely in the eye.

I said, "I still respect you, Landry." Then I went to a stall in the lavoratory and cried. Landry was in Haiti with her mother when Mr. Pope put a gun to his mouth, and they never returned to New Orleans.

Country Day is an American Eton. It's bully. Actually, the school's official name is Metairie Park Country Day, but it's been called Country Day since a group of Uptown parents decided to launch, on a fourteen-acre campus, a school that would "give students not only competence in academics, but confidence in all those other skills so important to a successful life." That was in 1929. The stately columned brick administration building was purposely designed to resemble what it most looks like: a private house. The architecture underscores the school's family atmosphere. All of the twenty or so buildings are surrounded by flower gardens, sweeping green lawns, and open playing fields. Country Day took us from Lower School (K–6), to Middle School (7–8) and, finally, to Upper School (9–12).

We were schooled before the lion had lain with the lamb. Before sternness and justice became "I wish to be your friend." Schools wouldn't be in such total collapse if there were more iron fists in velvet gloves. Who wants a headmaster to be one's friend? Mutual respect is what one wants.

Anyway, Mother's decline started with Papa's death. She just never got over it. She was only thirty-eight, but she was dead too. Several years later Papa's brother, Fulton, was reminiscing about Papa's grace and his form on the tennis court while he was still in his teens and how the sun made a halo around his blond head, when Mother hoarsely told him to shut up. She then excused herself and did not come out of her room for a week.

No one could ever measure up. I most of all.

Burdensome it was, but I never wished them to have been mortal.

I really do digress. I think all Southerners do. Really must control myself. The past can eat you up. But we did have fun. It was like a great fair. You loved your friends and usually saw them every day. There was never an unfamiliar name. Had we been asked, or even had we thought, tomorrow could only be as happy as today had been. I never really knew an unhappy day until Papa died.

But this was still to come. Stebo and Baby were holding court in the Broadwater Beach

Hotel's lobby bar. No two people ever loved an audience more. Baby, all of eight years old, was perched on the marbled-topped walnut bar eating maraschino cherries from an iced bowl by her side. She had been born beautiful, but now she was a vision in white linen. The most glamorous thing I had ever seen. The ever-vigilant Otis was pleading with her to get down ... to sit lady-like in a chair, and to stop ruining her gloves:

"I don't want my fingers sticky."

"I don't want to get down."

"I don't want to sit in a chair."

"This marble is cool. It's keeping me from wrinkling," she said, oh so self-satisfiedly.

"Don't be bothering Miss Baby, Otis," Stebo barked. "I don't want My Baby being hot."

That settled, Baby then pressed another cherry to the suddenly most perfect pink lips I had ever seen.

Seeing me with Papa, Baby turned from Otis to welcome us.

"Come sit on the bar with me, Suddie. I'll give you one of my nice and cold maraschino cherries."

"What did you call me, Baby?" No one had ever called me "Suddie."

"Suddie. I called you Suddie," she ever so sweetly replied.

"No one's ever called me that, Baby." My heart was beating funny.

"Well, I'm not just anyone, as you should know by now, Sudduth Meadows Spencer. Now, come on up here and keep me company while

11

our handsome daddies talk. Don't you like cherries? I know you like me. Like me a lot. I can always tell when boys like me. Afternoon, Mr. Spencer. You sure are handsome. Just like my daddy."

Papa smiled and courtly half-bowed to Baby.

"Baby's certainly on her way to becoming a heart-breaker, Stebo," Papa remarked. "She's already a beauty."

"My small queen may break as many hearts as she wishes," Stebo answered proudly. "Beauty has privilege, Raiford. You and Arabella must know that."

"Suddie!" Baby says again.

I looked up at Papa. He shook his head. Baby saw him shake his head.

"Well, then I'll dance for you, Suddie. My daddy loves for me to dance just for him. But this time I'll dance just for you."

Baby then jumped up and began pirouetting, her dress twirling out.

Otis resumed his pleading. No one was paying him any mind.

Baby concluded her saucy dance by leaning over and kissing me right smack on my mouth. Right then I had my first and only religious experience. I wanted to fight off all comers for her. Defend her. Rescue her from mortal peril. I mean, I was violently in love. The incense from my worship would make me wish for nothing else in life and dimmed my eyes for those merely mortal. I was ten years old.

My name is Sudduth Meadows Spencer. I am named for my second cousin, Sudduth Meadows Ball, who died from asthma when he was twelve or thirteen. We have a huge portrait of him at the house. Mother inherited it because I resembled him, but Great-uncle Jonathan left all his money to the Asthma Foundation. Sudduth's sister had died of asthma, too. She had been ugly, so a portrait was never done.

But I must be getting back to Miss Fanny, who was now the Widow Soniat. Miss Fanny's "long and interesting silence" ended about two minutes after Steamboat Ravenal Soniat had been placed out in Metairie Cemetery under the Bishop-blessed marble angel for which Baby had posed. Baby was unceremoniously informed that she was not going to spend the rest of her life sunning the backs of her legs at the country club. That she had better decide on a major other than proms, parties, and popularity, because when she was graduated from Newcomb she would have two choices: to marry or to go to work. Miss Fanny was pulling in the reins because now she controlled the money and Baby's trust. That was just the beginning.

Miss Fanny had no intention of continuing to provide a setting for Baby. She was selling the Richmond Place house as well as the cottage and moving to Highlands, North Carolina where, for generations, Uptowners, living in secluded enclaves on Satolah Mountain, have enjoyed its small town charms and glorious alp-like air. Miss Fanny was sick to death of the Garden of Eden City, the weather, voodoo, jazz

13

funerals, and, most of all, of Baby, "the most worthless white child ever birthed."

With that, she marched out the front door and kept marching. All over town. Stopping people—even strangers. Miss Fanny was finally having her first breakdown, people said. (In New Orleans, one isn't considered normal unless one has had at least one breakdown—preferably in public. It's common knowledge that the sound of an owl could set Gladys de Gray off for weeks.) Hell, Miss Fanny hadn't had a breakdown; she was having her revenge. She had been plotting it for years.

Baby never complained and never explained. It was as if Miss Fanny were dead too. It was Baby's bravery that made even those who disapproved of her want to pet her. People thought of her as an orphan. She was inundated with invitations, invitations that would harbinger the peripatetic pattern to her new life. She was seventeen, an Education major now, and she never spent a weekend at the Kappa House except by choice.

You see, Baby wore valiancy well. Mainly because she had crushable bones. She was a swan with these wonderful bones. Bones that a man's hand could easily crush and just as easily kill for. No one ever had smaller wrists and such delicate long-fingered hands. Hands born to bestow colors on a knight off to battle and to play ivory-keyed pianos in flower-filled rooms during after-dinner coffee and brandy. Her hair was a bounty of newly minted gold coins. It was hair that made a man's hands itch and

14

sweat because it was hair a man wants a woman to have. She was an angel child and a devil woman, who had been born to be worshiped and violated.

As to whether Jane Jewel Dupree Parker or Baby had the most beautiful back in New Orleans, I'll answer, they both did. Each had a shimmering silver-white back, but Baby had flirtatious shoulders. Shoulders that were accentuated by strapless gowns worn to the balls in the cold and cavernous Municipal Auditorium. I can still see her being escorted to the floor from the call-out section by a committee man, her swan-like neck tossed back, and, on being presented to her masker, looking up at him as if he were God Almighty.

I miss Jane Jewel. She and Jolly Parker have been dead a long time. They were out on Lake Pontchartrain trying to conceive when the "Jolly Times" went down in a squall. But I'm digressing again.

While Papa's death ended Georgetown University and a Foreign Service career, life was still pleasant. The Days of the Raj were over, too, but Tulane was next door to Baby. If things were slipping away, no one noticed. Things have such a way of just dwindling away, don't they? Just dwindling away until all those things taken for granted, one day, are gone. We took so many things for granted, and now the whole of life is entirely different and no longer imperishable. Glory touched us for the first and last time.

Then, the world was at our feet. Now, it is at our throats.

Baby became a legend during these outré years. "Cry Havoc" was her mantra. Life just erupted around her.

Tarr (Bubba) Estes nearly killed me after I broke his nose at the country club defending Baby. Several years later my nose would be broken at the country club during my breakdown, but that was still to come.

Bubba's family was big rich new money. Besides being our state wrestling champion, Bubba had recently been ranked number one by the NCAA. At Country Day, he had been a national champion. Bubba was as dull as soil conservation. However, the fact that his parents had bought the Soniat houses and had had the effrontery to redo them in Himalayan awfulness made him anathema to Baby.

It was the evening of Betsy Barstow's coming out and Bubba was a hound dog scenting fox. I had determinedly ignored his umpteen taps on my shoulder to cut in, when Baby shouted, just as René (he was the Lester Lanin of New Orleans and was just as good, maybe better) stopped playing, and her voice carried over the ballroom.

"Get away from us, Bubba Estes. Leave me alone. You may be the sauce for somebody's goose, but I don't think you'll ever be worth a gander."

Well, Bubba took this with all the glowing

good humor of a tundra. He went to strike her. I interceded. Her pearls were suddenly pouring over the floor. My fist missed his jaw and broke his nose, the blood splattered. Between screaming, "Kill him, Suddie," Baby also screamed, "Be careful! Those are my great-grandmother's pearls!" She was totally oblivious to the fact that he was killing me. She still is. Bubba fights dirty. Does to this day, they say. I had three broken ribs and a ringing in my left ear for two years. As a result of this, his parents, who were up for club membership, were lastingly blackballed and Bubba's name struck from every list in town save one.

"Isn't It Romantic," that dreamy elegant legacy from Messrs. Rodgers and Hart, invokes that evening far better than those instant-replay memory machines now mesmerizing the public.

Baby was a great comforter. She was born knowing how to make a man feel ten feet tall. I was on the floor (Bubba had been pulled off and told to leave) with my head nestling her bosom that was the sweetness of life. *Douceur de vivre*, as the French would say. Those peerless breasts delighting me as always. She was kissing me, murmuring low, and pressing champagne to my mouth.

Pain evaporated. I pulled myself up. We danced as René played on. A dead man would have risen for Baby. It was the height of human happiness. But happiness can be as ephemeral as beauty and fame.

Days later we quarreled and did not speak for six weeks.

She called.
"Come play, Suddie."
Silence.
"Please."
"No."
"Don't be mean. I'm sorry. Please, I miss you. Come play with Baby."

I went to play. I always went to play. Right to the end.

My emotional promiscuity began the first time we played. I was nineteen and Stebo had been dead a year, I realized later. Actually, it was a year the morning we left and a year and two days when it happened. We were driving back from Biloxi. The house party had started out fun, but had ended in three breakdowns, one attempted suicide, and two jealous fights, not over Baby. She had been subdued for once.

I was thinking about Papa and the yellow Ford station wagon and the god awful house new people had put up on the property we once owned. William Alexander Percy was always writing about lanterns on the levee. I was thinking about ghosts on the lawn and the traditional rituals of pre-plastic summers. Of wet bathing suits drying. Of the swing Papa rigged up for me out of hemp rope and a left-over board from replaced front porch steps. Of how Mother padded the board to protect me from splinters. Of invariably knotted rubber garden hoses. Of Papa's black wool trunks that just naturally seemed to attract moths. Of his carrying clams in a galvanized tin pail. Of Mother cutting and arranging flowers in pastel eyelet dresses and

open-toed wedge shoes with heel straps. Of
Papa's freshly laundered, worn, seersucker suits
in the evening. Of my endlessly changed, but-
toned playsuits that caused me so much trouble
in the lavoratory. Of aimless happy laughter
and the postprandial chatter of guests on the
lawn as twilight died. Of mint juleps sweating
in Jefferson cups and how cool it felt to stand
by Papa, seated in one of the white Adirondack
lawn chairs, and rub my wrist against the cup.

Most of all, I was remembering the absolute
security of Papa and Mama's love for each other
and me.

"But, Papa, I'm not tired. I'm just resting
my eyes," as he carried me to bed, and being
asleep before arriving.

Of Mother and Papa coming in to kiss me
goodbye on their way to a dance. Of Papa leaning down to kiss me and retucking the covers.
Of Mother looking at herself in my bureau
looking glass and remarking out loud to herself:

"I'm beginning to age. I look old tonight.
Yes, I'm definitely losing my bloom."

Of Papa quickly straightening up and turning to her and saying:

"Darlin', you look the same to me as you did
the first time I saw you in your parents' front
hall when I looked and saw you coming down
the stairs."

Of Mother looking up at him and saying:

"Oh, Raiford, you are sweet. How could I
ever love anyone but you."

Of their kissing and leaving. Of feeling very
melancholy.

"What do you think about Suzanna's attempt to scare Dickie into behaving?" Baby asked me.

I switched off Fats Domino's wailing rendition of "I'm Walkin' to New Orleans" and turned:

"Nothing. That's what I think. Trying to drown herself by driving Dickie's Thunderbird into the Gulf of Mexico is not going to stop his fooling around. Suzanna knew he was a chronic chaser when she ran off with him. Now she's acting like white trash and he's no better, especially now that she's pregnant. Hell, I'm worn out. Trashed out. I'll be glad to get home. How about you?"

She said nothing.

"The night's startin' to settle in. The day is dying. Look, honey, there's the first star. I'll let you have it for a wish."

She said nothing.

"Darlin'? You sick? What's wrong? You've acted funny all weekend."

"You smell like sweat, smoke, and bourbon, just like Daddy," she said from far away. "Let's play. You want to play? Let's finally do it."

"Sheeiitttt!"

I nearly ran off the road.

"Well, at least say something besides that awful word, Sudduth Meadows Spencer," she hotly demanded. "Here I am offering you my beautiful white, young, and virgin body and all you can say is that really awful word. You have those things in the glove compartment. I checked when we stopped for gas back there and you got out."

She pushed her sunglasses up into her hair. Her blue eyes were strangely cold.

"Your sense of timing is bizarre, Baby. Here, I had envisioned. . . . "

"Don't be such a romantic, Suddie. Will you or won't you?"

She started to untie her madras wrap-around skirt and kicked off her espadrilles.

I kissed her eyes, her mouth, her neck and said "Don't, Baby. Wait. Let me."

Later, I was spiraling as I moved, as if I were trapped in the center of a tornado, being flung toward Oz at the end of the physical rainbow. It was like elation and a kick from the devil at the same time.

Baby moaned, "Jesus Chr. . . . O Jesus! Dadddeee. . . . Dadddeee. . . . Stebo. . . . Steboooo!"

I waited for her eyes to open and asked, "Is it so hard to love me?"

She said nothing.

The prancing fun of our school years was like a brilliant fireworks display before which the stars for a moment paled. Before the glory ended, five of our group would never grow old. They were the lucky ones.

Daisy, who glowed like a nectarine in a sheltered garden, drowned. Hurst, whose giant-sized heart loved jazz so passionately, died from, of all things, a ruptured appendix. Alice and Paulette, known as the A&P twins, with their sultry faces and glorious energy, burned in a chartered plane along with their mother and father; and Toby, who lived on the crest of laughter, was crushed to death in his sports car at a red light by a tree that was felled in a freak storm.

For us, who lived on, it was endless nights in a jazz jungle where sweat on hot nights is something alive. It was dance, dance, dance and the air redolent with chocolate, chicory coffee, and oleander as we drove up St. Charles Avenue with the sun breaking over the still mighty oaks and palms. The echoing of our laughter mingled with the clanking of the streetcar bringing maids to Uptown houses and, on its return trip, fathers to downtown offices.

We knew the Avenue then as well as we knew the welcoming doors of the houses along its way. The Avenue led to everything. It was a pulsating artery.

Baby fell in love with kites during these, the prancing years. In the heaviness of a New Orleans evening, some fellow would drive her up and down the Avenue in a convertible, her kite flying gaily in the breeze. For a time, Baby wouldn't know anyone who didn't own a convertible.

Hopeful beaux began making kites to gain her favor. Their life expectancy was short for she abandoned a kite as quickly as she did a heart. Kites resemble soaring hearts, and it was wrenching to see them cast off in a gutter or left mangled on the sidewalk outside Fat Harry's Bar.

I never made her a kite.

Kit Kat Carson and I were flirting on the terrace at Southern Yacht Club the night Baby suddenly appeared and accusingly asked me why I was the only boy who hadn't made her a kite.

I told her I didn't have a convertible and walked away. I thought I might vomit.

* * *

2

"What's it all about, Alfie?" I said to myself as I pondered the meaning of life on the morning I was graduated from Tulane armed with a degree in English and a super tan. Our tropical rain had drowned Mother's most insouciant summer hat, and she was cross all day. Even the knowledge that about a hundred people said she was prettier than any girl in my class didn't elevate her mood.

Was this prophetic of life beyond the halls of ivy? Right then I decided to go to graduate school after Mother and I returned from Europe. My graduation present was to be a two-month Grand Tour. We sailed on the mighty Cunard Queens, Mary and Elizabeth. Now this was splendor and majesty. It was a history-making time to sail because it was the first time in Cunard's existence that weekly departures could be sailed in each direction by the liners. All that luxury is gone now. Even from planes and trains. Yes, one gets everywhere faster, but one might as well be in a cattle car.

We were in that park-like district of Berlin, the Grunewald, breakfasting in the garden of the Schloss Gehrhus, when Mother called me Raiford for the first time. (The Grunewald is to Berlin what Uptown is to New Orleans and for the most part escaped Allied bombing.)

Everyone knows Thomas Wolfe said, "You can't go home again." Well, you can't go back to the SAE house either where the only rule had been to be in bed by 4:00 A.M. if playing tennis.

It was a mistake to return. I realized I had had my time, and a merry time it had been. Let others have theirs. They did. But they never had as much fun. I left at the end of the term.

Money was also becoming tiresome.

One morning Mr. Crushank rang. He was always Mr. Crushank. I don't think he had a first name. Anyway, he was a trust officer with the Whitney Bank. He wanted us to come downtown. Mother said she didn't go downtown anymore.

"Couldn't you come for breakfast? I'll have Frances do pork chops and pecan waffles. They were always Mr. Spencer's favorite. Yes, 9:30 would be fine."

Money should never be discussed at table.

In essence, he said the money was galloping away and stressed the need to canter from here on.

Mother replied: "Gallop? Canter? Do you ride, Mr. Crushank?"

I told Mr. Crushank to give Mother half the money in my trust, which wasn't that much anymore, and that day seriously started to look for a job.

A month later, Oliver Carrebee IV hired me after Dagg Hillyer and I won a doubles tournament at the Lawn Tennis Club, the oldest tennis club in the United States, I might add.

We were walking off the court when Mr. Carrebee called to me from the gallery.

"You play well, Sudduth. Very good back hand."

"Thank you, Sir."

"Perhaps Dagg wouldn't mind if you have a drink with me? I have a proposition for you."

"No, Sir," said Dagg.

"Sudduth?"

"Yes, Sir. I'm mighty thirsty."

I walked up the stairs. Mr. Carrebee had inherited Carrebee Business Publications and ran it from a fine old building on Carondelet Street. The remnants of his good looks had been blurred by too much drinking and eating. He was gruff, but very paternal. I liked him.

"Sudduth, why haven't you been to see me?"

"Well, Sir, I did drop by your personnel office. Was told there were no openings and that an English degree wouldn't be of much value in business publications."

"You should have come to see me, boy! Raiford and I were Phi Delt at Auburn. Your father was a fine man. Damn shame about him dying so young. Your mama needs to get about more. Arabella's too pretty...."

"Yes, Sir, I know."

"Listen, I want you to come work for me. Be the youngest editor I have. The editor of my textile magazine died Thursday."

"Textiles? I do need a job, Mr. Carrebee, but I'll be honest with you, I don't know anything about cotton except we once had people who picked it before the War."

(In the South, there has only been one war.)

"Well, at least you're honest and think right. Don't worry about that, you'll learn. Anyway, I'll wager an unnatural fiber has never touched your body, and the advertisers' wives will be crazy for you."

"Where do wives come in?"

"At conventions. At receptions. At invitations for weekends that will come. If the wives like you, the husbands like you. That's how big contracts are signed. It's done offhand. Say at the end of a visit, you'll be told: 'Have Murray, (Murray Stein was the New York rep) call me about six double-page spreads' or...'about renewing next fall's contract.' Understand?"

I nodded.

"There's an associate editor to check verbs, commas, and spelling. If you were thinking about New York and high-tone books, well not only don't they pay, they'd chew you up, and you weren't meant to starve or be poor. Know why?"

"No, Sir."

"Because you're a gentleman, Sudduth. There's nothing wrong with being a gentleman and you were born one just like your pa. There's just not much calling for gentlemen today. Most people, and by that, Sudduth, I mean the 'not our kinds of people' who are taking over, won't understand or appreciate a gentleman. Look at the Avenue. There's rumors that the people who bought the Nicholson Perry house did so with Mafia money. Paid cash. From a suitcase. There, you're young. You'll learn. Maybe I'll have better luck with you than I did with my boys. Real shame you weren't able to go to Georgetown. Foreign Service would have suited you."

There are no secrets in Uptown.

"How about it? You going to work for me?"

"Yes, Sir."

"Fine. Be in my office Monday at ten. After that the hours are 9:00–4:30 and I like my people to have business lunches. Don't worry, the company pays."

"Thank you, Mr. Carrebee. Monday it is."

"Sudduth, isn't there anything you wish to ask me?"

"Sir?"

"Money, boy! See what I mean about New York? Don't worry. I won't take advantage of you. I already like you better than my own boys."

He never did take advantage. And he did like me better.

The Carrebees had three sons. The youngest, a drinker, lived in the Quarter with a black woman. He received a monthly check to stay there. The second son's monthly check was sent to Germany. He had been sent there following a series of unusual experiences that began with

29

his expulsion from Valley Forge Military Academy for something to do with sheep, and later from Culver, for something to do with the entire drill team, and finally from the Marine Corps for something to do with two privates and a captain. With all that military training and his natural proclivity for uniforms, Germany seemed the perfect place for him. The oldest son, who occupied the office next to his father, hated me.

Oliver Carrebee started me at $12,500 a year. It was the spring of 1966. I was twenty-three years old. Over the next nine-month period I received three $500 raises.

I had arrived promptly at ten that first Monday morning. By eleven, the head of personnel had taken me to a place to get a social security card. At noon, Mr. Carrebee and I were lunching at the Carrebee table in Galatoire's, the table I would use for future business lunches.

For me, lunching at Galatoire's on a weekday was a first. While anytime is the time to go, the only real time is Sunday. From noon to sometimes even seven, fading mirrors reflect an aristocracy of elegance united by private memories even more deeply rooted than inbred consanguinity, holding court at tables draped with dazzling white cloths and set with heavy silver.

Galatoire's, where tourists and others wait in long queues and pay cash. No credit cards accepted. Galatoire's, where old-line families walk in to be escorted to table by waiters more like family retainers after so many generations, and where they are billed on the first of the month.

On occasion, the queue people will glare

and mutter in low tones. I always smile at them, think of God, Grace, and Grandfather, and say:

"I'm a guest. A very late one, too. Excuse me."

Some forgive me.

Others, they will kill with their eyes.

"Don't you dare look at me that way. I certainly don't need to explain to you my reason for not having to stand in line."

On bad days, when my clock strikes twelve and stops, it's at Galatoire's that one can see Jackie and Walter Bolton laughing and waving to friends. Jackie born to wear a hat and not owning one that doesn't complement her beauty.

Longer de la Gueronniere, the debonair French Count, his pipe clinched firmly between his teeth, admiring and making love to all women with his eyes.

Ruth, his spirited wife. Her large melting eyes greeting friends with "Darling! How you doing, kid? Longer and I are having a few people over later. Do come. We'll have fun, cutie pie." Ruth's superb seat, on even a poor hunter, is perfection. No matter how late she and Longer have partied, she is always animated and sleek in her de rigueur veil and smart black habit.

At their elegant 1851 house on Esplanade Avenue, with its steel shutters and cast-iron railings set between paneled box columns, it was always fine food, fine wine, and fine times. (Esplanade Avenue was one of the most beautiful streets in New Orleans. It was where one saw creole beauty and society at its best and was to the Creoles what St. Charles Avenue was to us.)

31

Hillyer Speed Lamkin, the novelist/playwright, flying in from Monroe but reeking Saville Row and Dunhill and "still the thinnest person in my class from Harvard."

"Listen, try Swiss Miss. I know. Yeah, I owe this trim body to Swiss Miss. How's Marguerite? She's fine. Yeah, she had dinner at Buck House last Friday. What's Buck House? Drop dead."

The chicly, classical, size-zero Francophile, Margie Davis, and her husband, Walter, who's just about the bravest man in the state. He was shot through the head defending Margie. They have the largest private art collection in the city. Modigliani. Gainsborough. O'Keefe.

Carol Layton Parsons, flying in from Europe, Bryn Mawr, or Layton Castle, the only one in Louisiana. In this truly feudal structure, the ballroom occupies the main tower. Carol lives for culture. "The art was fabulous. We went behind the scenes at every major museum. Five weeks on a bus is madness but it was worth it. The group was darling. I just loved them, especially the Duchess of Portland. She was my roommate."

The fabled Alice Foster Lynch. Alice has enjoyed every moment of her life and loves a good story. "I adore it. It's the funniest thing I ever heard. I adore it."

Pierrot Villere, former Queen of Carnival, whose dismissive look for the world included most of all her daughter, Little Pierrot, with her latest widower. "Don't take this wrong, Gil darling, it's just that you were more attractive in Palm Beach."

Ellen Gander, whom everybody has called Goosey since Country Day, unable to eat for table-hopping.

Owen Johnson, the attorney/genealogist, and a cousin, back from a speaking engagement, having fun with the very soignée Helen Marie Martell.

The stunning Trimbles. One half of New Orleans thinks he's the better looking, while the other half thinks she is.

The grand dame Percy Sue Kerr Hyams, the Grinling Gibbons of using doors for paneling.

The always beautiful Jane Louise Clemenceau and her husband Pierre, who has published, in French, the biography of his grandfather, Georges Clemenceau, the premier of France during World War I. Pierre has all the Gallic charm of Maurice Chevalier, but is better looking.

Violetta Judell, with her Castillian grandee ancestry's pride in *pureza de la sangre* antedating the conquest of Spain, drop-dead looking in pink from hat to shoes.

Drake Monroe, throwing bread at Carter Ray's adored wife, and her screaming, "Don't! Stooooop!" but loving the attention.

And, Baby...most of all Baby. Baby, bussing everyone and eating from their plates. For Baby, everyone's plate is always greener.

By two, Mr. Carrebee and I had returned and I was in a private office facing a huge roll-top desk that still contained the belongings of my dead predecessor, and was having what I would later understand to be an anxiety attack. I wanted to run away. I wanted to die. I wanted to climb in Mack's lap and bury my head in her skinny bosom and be told everything would be all right.

"Child, don't you fret, Mack's here. She'll make things right."

Desdemona Mack had made things right for generations of Uptown babies before her retirement. Tall and skinny as a rail, her standards of conduct were frequently higher than those of the families for whom she worked.

Mack's standards never capitulated. Never.

Once, when a Heartbreaker Chi Omega whom I had met at an Ole Miss football weekend in Oxford invited me to Beverly Hills for a visit the following June, I went.

Football was shining, noble, and all-consuming then. Being seated with a dozen couples in good seats, snug and secure under a heavy old lap robe, was the closest thing to heaven on earth. A bourbon-filled flask in one's jacket that perhaps would make a pretty young thing's hands wander was the essence of "What's it all about, Alfie?"

"Well, just a sip, Suddie. It is soooo cold."

"Honey, take two, at least. Maybe three. I don't want you catchin' a chill." I was a sly devil, or so I thought.

A giggle would follow each swallow.

"God, honey, your hands are freezing. Here, put them under the blanket. I'll warm them in my lap."

"Promise not to be bad?"

"Of course, darlin'. Would I be bad with the Sweetheart of Sigma Chi?"

"I don't know. Mama says nice girls keep both hands on top of the blanket. Why are you looking at me so hard, Suddie?"

"Because I'm afraid you'll disappear. You're just so pretty that I don't think you're really here."

"Well, I'll just put one hand under for now."

And the tailgate parties in the fall. G&T's, Madras jackets, hampers of fried chicken and, just before the first cold spell, homecoming and corsages and cheering for people one knew.

I have absolutely no interest in football today. Haven't for years.

Anyway, I went to California. Had a super time. But I certainly wouldn't ever live there. I never met so many iconoclastic people in my life. Budding Heartbreaker's parents lived not far from the house where Gloria Swanson seduced and later shot William Holden in *Sunset Boulevard.* Remember, the film opens with him floating face down in this swimming pool. The house was now owned, but very seldom lived in, by a "freak" from Chicago. (That's the term Heartbreaker's father used.) The freak was the founder of this religious cult who believed James Dean was God. He and his followers worshiped James Dean. See what I mean about California. Heartbreaker and I ambled over one day when the wind was up and a nauseating smell coming from the house was driving people back into theirs. We discovered the stench was the stagnated water in the swimming pool. Instead of a floating face-down William Holden, there were dead animals, birds, and a partially submerged canoe just rotting away.

Well, anyway, in having such a super time I spent all my money. This included turning in my airplane ticket. When it was time to come home, I called Mother. I was more than ready. I missed New Orleans and I had had enough of Heartbreaker and California. Mother was not amused by my news, but said she would send another ticket and some money. She did too. A Greyhound bus ticket. The trip could have been grim, but gregarious soul that I am, I formed fast friendships similar to ones formed on a transatlantic crossing. We arrived at the New Orleans bus terminal around five-thirty in the morning. I was bidding adieu, exchanging addresses, and shaking hands when I heard:

"Hey, looker there. That must be one of them mammys I've heard tell about, and she's gettin' on! She looks madder than hell."

I didn't have to turn around, but I did. I just wanted to be invisible. To be anywhere but there.

A white-uniformed Mack charged toward me like an avenging angel. Shit. She didn't even work for us anymore, but Mother's punishments were always very well thought out.

"Here I was thinking of you as a practically grown man. You ought be real ashamed of yourself. Spending all your money. Coming home just like trash. That's right, Mr. Sudduth. Just like white trash."

Nobody was laughing.

"Where your things? Hurry up. I got a United

cab outside and he ain't too pleased about waiting. Miss Bella didn't want her car brought down here. People get killed here. Don't you know that? This here is a bad place. I'm ashamed to even be seen, not that I would know anybody."

"Did you get my postcard, Mack?"

"Yes, but I threw the thing away. Only crazy peoples and trash of all kinds live in Hollywood. You ready? We going home. What you looking at, Woman? Mind your own business. You hear me? I smack you good, Gal. Ain't you ever seen quality?"

Mack was truly a dedicated snob, the greatest who ever lived.

It was also Mack (not even in jest would she answer to Desdemona) who had given me one of the worst whippings I ever had. You see, she liked to show off her charges and did so by taking them with her to the Gethsemane Temple Church. So I, dressed in my best white sailor suit, with Mack in her Sunday best, was taken to church to be shown off. When she caught me stealing cookies from a black child who was a slow eater at the social hour following the service (I've always had a weakness for cookies), she carried me to the lavoratory and wore me out, crying the entire time about how I had shamed her. And here deftly ended what could have become a life of petty crime.

Mack had once been married to a "light skinned" male who made her sing "the black man blues."

"I finally had to shed myself of him," she'd sigh. "You see, I was a front door woman, and he was a back door man. But when the wind's up and the trees they be moaning, I sure do miss that big sweet hunk of trash."

It took me three months to become acclimated to working, another three to feel secure, and another three to realize I had returned to a womb.

The interior of Carrebee's was, in retrospect, an extension of my grandparents' house and reflected the best taste of their day. It had last been decorated in 1913, in the post-Edwardian grandeur of massive mahogany and oak. There was no sheet rock, plywood, or Formica. There were honest-to-God brass spittoons. The next youngest editor was forty-three, and the employees were a collection of Uptown's poorer second and third cousins, minor debutantes who had failed to be auctioned off, three granddaughters of two former governors, two sons of former mayors, forgotten sports heroes, and one former all-American fullback who had slept with Clara Bow and Joan Crawford. Everyone was either Miss, Mrs., or Mr. and related as only one can be in the South, or had attended the same schools, or had belonged to the same fraternity or sorority.

The most beloved person was my associate editor. She taught me more than all my expensive education ever did. An orphan, her great love was opera. I had been working for three years when she up and disappeared during opera week. Mr. Carrebee even hired detectives when the police failed to come up with anything. The detectives traced her to New York City. She was living near Lincoln Center with a soprano famous for the role of Mimi in "La Boheme." They are still together. Every Christmas, she sends me a card.

The most unusual person, to say the least, was a "maiden lady," who was a first cousin of Oliver's wife. Miss Callie was a little woman with a big voice. Dripping wet she couldn't have weighed over ninety pounds. Miss Callie kept her face, neck, and arms packed with rice powder from Japan and dyed her sixty-seven strands of hair with iodine straight from the bottle. I think all that iodine must have affected her brain. Her office was down the hall from mine and was choked with elephant ears and banana trees that she cursed most of the day. These plants just thrived on verbal abuse. Conversation was limited to "Morning," "Afternoon," and "Night." All day Miss Callie cursed, smoked, and sipped gin for her "sinking spells" from a silver hip flask routinely refilled, by means of a much-coveted-by-me silver funnel, from a half-gallon of gin she kept behind her open office door. Now Miss Callie rarely had a good day, but when she did, one really felt happy for her. When Dolph Plummer didn't reply to her "good day" greeting one morning in the hall, she turned around and yelled at him:

"You goddamn pygmy son-of-a-bitch, when I speak to you, you better goddamn well reply. Hell, I've known you since you were a Baptist. Since before you converted and married up."

39

Actually, Miss Callie was from a lovely family. She had been Queen of Eros in her youth. What changed her, no one knew. One year just before Christmas, her final breakdown occurred. One of the associate editors had crafted two wreaths for the inner lobby doors. Miss Callie became overwhelmed by their beauty. As she exclaimed, they were the "goddamnedest most beautiful wreaths she had ever seen. Goddamn, yes they were." She must have taken the Lord's name in vain about three hundred times. She just wouldn't shut up. Someone went to fetch her flask in hopes that a quick shot would calm her, but it was too late. Miss Callie up and dropped dead right in the middle of our lobby with a cigarette in her mouth.

In actuality, it was a terrible place for me, it was the best place for me. When, seventeen years later, the heirs sold all the magazines to a Chicago corporation and the building was razed for a high-rise development, I felt like Mickey Rooney leaving Boys Town forever, and with good reason. Carrebee took care of its own. All those years and I had never been in a bank, much less done my own income tax. Bookkeeping handled everything.

I came to thrive in this gingerbread atmosphere and, just as Oliver Carrebee had predicted, the invitations were eventually forthcoming, as were the contracts. If the wives became too serious, I had a line that saved us both.

"I think we might be breaking the rules. We both know it's bad form to be serious."

In time, I revamped my magazine and won

three publishing awards. Oliver was very proud. He made me an officer.

I moved to an apartment the day I turned twenty-four. Times they were a-changin'. The next year, a sweet and slinky Baby was graduated from Newcomb, and Mother became even more withdrawn with the deaths of Frances and Daniel. They had been mainstays, family, and links to better days.

"Francesca de Bestest" and "Daniel in the Lion's Den", I had "petted" them years before. Frances, the best and only one-armed cook in Uptown, and Daniel, her husband and our houseman, who loved to make things shine.

Mack returned to live with Mother. Much aged and with bad eyes. She and Mother would just chat away about good blood, bad blood, old blood, and new blood as they polished the silver and all the while a chinchilla of dust covered the furniture. For someone whose education ended at age eleven, Mack knew more about New Orleans, Natchez, and Charleston bloodlines than most professional genealogists. Their other topic of conversation was whether Papa or I had been the better looking baby. Mother finally conceded I was the prettier baby, but Papa the more handsome man.

"Six feet, four inches is the only height for a man," Mother has always maintained.

I am six feet tall.

Soon, the well-bred ivy which upholstered the house forgot itself and ran wild, and the front door brass was no longer polished every day. Is there anything more abandoned than an unpolished door knocker? An unpolished door knocker says it all. Think about it. For what it proclaims for all to see is: "Pass on. My time is past."

* * *

3

Baby departed Newcomb

in a blaze of glory, but unengaged and without any brilliant marriage prospects.

Why, people asked.

Had any girl ever been so popular or hotly chased?

Had anyone ever had such an illustrious season?

New Orleans has always had the world's longest debutante season, August to Ash Wednesday. Girls far less pretty and popular were engaged to or marrying Baby's rejects.

"I'm too young for marriage," she'd laugh when asked.

"Life is too short to be tied down."

"Maybe next year."

Then came: "I'll marry when I run out of money."

Baby had become flush when Aunt Valkyrie, and her husband, Siegfried, were asphyxiated in their State Street house along with their cook, Rita, three dogs, two cats, and a bird. Childless and hating Miss Fanny, they left everything to Baby. (Actually, they had two hates. The other was Wagner.)

"Prostrate with grief," Baby arranged nine funerals. ("God," she moaned, "all that was missing was a partridge in a pear tree!") She then lunched with the president of the gas company to discuss the negligence of the work crew which had been repairing State Street gas lines, sold the house at top dollar, carefully picked over the furnishings and things she would keep, had Morton's auction the rest, and bought a condominium on the Avenue opposite Christ Church Cathedral.

The building's exterior was pink and white and everything nice. Almost like Baby. If people were saddened by the loss of the Second Empire, mansard-roofed, Flower's place, with its ornate porthole dormer windows and collapsing porte-cochere, its replacement, the condominium, at least had great style and wonderfully romantic balconies. The turn-of-the-century house had been built by Mayor Walter Flower, whose daughter, Marion, married the Count Henri de la Gueronniere, Longer's father, at a still-talked-about wedding. Longer's parents were at the Chateau Thouron, near Nautiers, France when World War II was declared and were detained there for the duration.

Baby's unit faced the Avenue for parade watching and while a Queen's flag should only be displayed during Carnival, she broke with tradition by hanging hers out to signify she was "at home." If her flag were out, it was party time, or as she would giggle, "Let's trash out."

When she bought a yellow Ford station wagon, I thought, in the words of Cole Porter, "Is it real turtle soup?—or only the mock? Or is it at long last love?" It was the mock.

With the money had come a new reply.

"I'll think about marrying after I return from England."

England was to be followed by every other known or unknown country or place. Just leave a space and fill it in.

The day came when she finally said what I knew she'd say one day. Fuck. She had been programmed for it! And here, an army of male names could be substituted.

"Marry Oakes? Don't be silly. He's just a boy. I'll marry a man like my daddy."

I went out and got blind drunk.

My apartment was up the Avenue from Baby's, just above Napoleon and below Josephine in a traditional Greek Revival. I was no stranger to the house. I had been to many parties here in the past. It had been a happy, beautiful house and, mercifully, had been cheeringly converted to four apartments when the last of the Grammonts had died the year before. I never failed to caress its curving rosewood banister whenever I went up or down the stairs. I didn't have a balcony, but I did have an enclosed screened gallery amply shaded on one side by two giant magnolias. Life was still pleasant and the good times rolled, but I missed the certainties that were gone and resented the restless dissatisfaction that had replaced them.

I felt like shit. Twenty-two thousand Chinese had probably died the night before feeling better than I did right then.

Baby's car horn made me jump from my hammock. It made everyone jump. It played "Mary Had a Little Lamb," which is rather prophetic considering how many lambs Baby led to slaughter.

"Unlock your door. I've come to visit," she yelled up.

"It's open," I shouted down. "Don't you believe in telephones?"

"Stop talking and fix us some drinks."

Pretty girls in white tennis dresses can kill a man, I thought as I mixed double vodka tonics.

"Here's to all the pretty girls at the Lawn Tennis Club this fine Saturday morning," I saluted. "To what do I owe the honor of this visit? Have you been pining for me or has Brockman become tiresome?"

"The prettiest girl at the club was me."

"Was I," I corrected.

"Pedantic prick."

"Sewer mouth."

"I'm sorry. I'll be sweet. Why didn't you play this morning?" she asked.

"I didn't feel much like it."

I got back in the hammock and she pushed an ottoman over to be nearer.

"How's the Double Queen? You even smell pretty." I pulled her hand to my lips and kissed her fingers and palm. "I don't know which is worse: being with you or not being with you. Why can't I be done with you?"

"Because you really love me."

"And, insensitive child that you are, you hurt the one who loves you best, Baby."

"I never mean to hurt you, Suddie."

"I know.... Life after school sucks. I miss those less complicated days and attachments. Do you?"

"Not really," she said. "I never miss anything except..."

"You never miss me?" I asked, not being interested in 'except' and already knowing 'except.'

"It's strange, Suddie, but with you, I just pretend you've gone to the lavoratory and are coming right back."

"Do you not think you carry honesty too far?"

"Well, I don't think about any of the others that way. So there," she said as if this truth absolved her.

"Thank you for the crumbs from your table, pet."

"Oh, Suddie, have I hurt you?"

"Do you still have my SAE pin?"

"Sugar Baby, I have everybody's SAE pin, as well as Sigma Chi, Sigma Nu, Phi Delt, KA, and Kappa Sig. I have two drawers full of them. When this aristocratic neck goes, the one you're always wanting to wrench, I'm going to have a gold neckband made and have it embedded with all those precious and semi-precious stones."

"You're a heartless bitch."

"Yes. I'll have them all melted down. All except for yours."

My heart jumped.

"Yours is in a special place. A secret place along with somebody else's."

"Whose somebody else's!"

"Ummmm."

This was her newest way of not answering questions. It was maddening. Sometimes, it was all I could do to keep from striking her.

"It's with Stebo's, isn't it?"

Her look answered my question and she turned away.

"Let's play," she said to the magnolias.

"No, thank you, pet. Not today. I don't feel like being a substitute."

"Are you saying I use you?"

"I'm not saying anything else. You just said it. I rest my case."

"Why can't we get along for over two minutes before we start to fight?" She said this as if it were all my fault.

"Because there's always Stebo between us, Baby."

"Well, I know all about your breaking the engagement off with Pandora and that Yankee advertiser's ugly daughter who tried to kill herself over you. So there. Was Oliver upset? No, I 'spect not. You're his fair-haired boy. No wonder Junior hates you. God, he has awful zits. Enough to make a soul puke! You know, his wife Cissa was my big sister when I went Kappa. Not pretty, but real sweet. She must have married him for his money. Had to. Remember, when they married, his face was worse then. Really, like an open sore."

"Shut up, honey."

"Come on, Suddie, let's play. You were the first, after all. Remember?"

I remembered.

"But not the last," I said.

"Bastard."

One day we'll kill each other, I thought.

"Well, will you or won't you?"

"Honey, I'm bad hungover."

"Well, I'm hungover, too, Suddie, but let's play anyway."

"We drink too much, Baby. We all drink too much."

"I'll promise ... "

"Promise what?"

"Promise not to drink too much, if you ... "

"I promise."

"Come on, let's play."

"What about Brockman?"

"Oh, I told him to go make me a kite and then go fly it."

"Cunt!"

"You know you love it. Let's play."

She jumped in the hammock.

* * *

4

The very air was sweating, and flowers, lush to the point of being overblown and slightly common, were dropping their petals the Sunday morning the *Times-Picayune* announced the engagement of Miss Baby Soniat to Mr. Taliaferro Eubanks Peabody. Uptown people were either rendered momentarily speechless or nearly choked to death on their Bloody Marys.

Taliaferro Peabody! Gooood God! There had to be some mistake. It was no mistake. It was Baby, and the announcement held the honored, top, left-hand-page position. However, if one took the time to notice, the photograph was no studio-posed portrait but a cropped picture from one of the many already on file.

Taliaferro, or "Tolerable" as he became quickly sobriqueted by Baby, wouldn't inspire a cricket to chirp. Don't get me wrong. I liked Tal. I had known him since our first days at Country Day. In an inchoate way I was even fond of him. No one could not like him.

All the Peabodys were well-liked. The fact that the great-grandfather who made all the money had been a carpetbagger had long been forgotten because they were so good, so quiet, and so rich.

Tal had been a change-of-life baby. He had the oldest parents in Uptown. He was thirty-four and his parents were over eighty.

I was having my third Bloody Mary when Baby rang.

"You know?" she inquired.

"Of course. Why?"

"I was tired and you weren't here to play with."

"Don't go putting the blame on me or I'll hang up."

"Well, you were away at some tacky place up North having a fine time!"

"One does not have a fine time at a textile convention in Atlantic City, as you should damn well know!"

"I'm sorry."

"Were you drunk?"

"What do you mean?"

"You know goddamn well what I mean!"

"No, damn you. But I was just a tad hungover."

"You swore. . . ."

"Suddie, please! I didn't do a thing. Truly! I was having a nectar soda at Smith's when he suddenly sat on the stool next to mine and asked what I was having. He had never had a nectar, so I told him to have a taste of mine and if he liked it I'd treat him to a double-deluxe. Can you believe that? Never had a nectar in his life. He must be the only boy.... "

"Baby, for Christ's sake!"

"Oh. Well, he had about two sips and the next thing I knew he was asking me to marry him. Just then I looked out the window and saw my car finally being booted for all those zillion unpaid tickets, so I said yes, burst into tears, and he promised to pay the tickets and get my car back."

"You'll ruin his life."

"I know. He has cocker spaniel eyes that are so appealing in a bitch, but deplorable in a man."

"What a bitch you are!"

"Yes, I am, but what shall I do?"

"That's your problem."

"Suddie, please!"

"Return the ring for starters."

"Return my ring! My ring cost over thirty-five thousand dollars."

"Since when did you become a whore?"

"Fuck you!"

You see, we have this fathomless capacity for hurting each other.

She did return the ring, but by then it was too late. It was at the engagement party.

You see, Baby's legend craved attention.

"It's almost like being Queen of Carnival again," she'd tell people.

And so it came to pass in a carpetbagger's ballroom, the second largest in New Orleans, that Stebo Soniat's pride and folly fell from grace and favor forever in front of assorted and re-pressed Peabodys and two hundred guests.

Wearing the Soniat pearls down her back with priceless carelessness, Baby was at the height of her estranging beauty. The soon-to-be uxorious Tal could only gulp and try to stay near her, but she distanced herself from him with wanton recklessness.

I had come by myself. It's a terrible thing to know a human nature too well. Baby was going to be a heroine for the first time in her life and, in doing so, write herself a tragedy. Baby's eyes were feral when Alabama and Claiborne approached to offer their congratulations.

Her reply stunned them and all those within hearing.

"You should be thanking me for not marry-ing Claiborne. You were just second choice, Alabama. Just about every girl here is married to one of my rejects. You all better be careful. Bet I could just snap my fingers and get them back."

Tal found his voice.

"Baby, please," Tal pleaded. "These are our friends. What's wrong? Why are you acting this way? Come on, darlin', let's dance. Miss Baby doesn't need any more champagne, Luther. Thank you."

"Don't go making decisions for me, Tolerable. Come on, boy, I'll dance with you, but not to that. For God's sake, René, this is a party, not *thé dansant!*"

"What would you like, Miss Soniat?"

"Something low-down!"

"Such as?"

"What about 'Birmingham Papa Your Memphis Mamma's Comin' To Town'?"

"Well...."

"Play it!"

"Yes, Miss Soniat."

Baby danced, but not with Tal.

She did a bump and grind that would have shamed a Bourbon Street stripper.

Mr. and Mrs. Peabody turned and left the room.

Baby's strapless gown was pulled briefly to her waist by Tal in an attempt to control her, and tiny sequins rained around them like stars. In an attempt to free herself, Baby cruelly bit Tal's hand and, stepping back, slapped him across his face.

"My daddy would have killed you for that!" Baby screamed. "I hate you, Tal! I'll hate you forever! Suddie, get me away from here. Suddie, where are you?" Seeing me, she ran to where I was standing at the back.

René was no longer playing.

"You want him to hate you? Don't you?" I demanded as we drove toward my apartment. "Answer me, damnit! You're not drunk."

"I want him to hate me forever," came as barely a whisper.

"Why?"

"His eyes."

"His eyes?"

"Yes. He is the only truly good person I ever knew. His eyes mirror his soul. He's too good for the likes of us."

I loved her beyond bearing. Beyond reason.

"Marry me, Baby! Marry me now! Fuck everybody. Fuck the world!"

"No. I'll never marry anyone. I can't marry anyone. I married my daddy years ago. You know that. You and Mama always knew. He loved me best. She hates me. My own mama really hates me. I wish I'd slept with him. I always wanted to. I still do. I used to watch him through the keyhole of his dressing room. He would be naked. No one would believe his body...."

"Shut up! Shut up or I swear to God I'll kill you."

I stopped the car and grabbed her.

"No one will ever love you the way I do. That endless legion of admirers wouldn't even like you, much less want you, if they knew the real you. Not even the mighty Stebo. Yes, that's right. Not even your precious Stebo. He loved ... goddamn it! Look at me! Stebo loved an untouched Snow Queen/child. I love a totally selfish, vain, thoughtless, psychotic child/bitch. Most people are self-centered, but you're a city in one. Stebo would never have touched you. Do you hear me? He 'pedestalized' his Snow Queen. That's why he pounced on anything that moved. You can't fuck a statue. You're ruining our lives mooning over a dead man who, if he were alive, would be a tired old man."

She cried all the way up the Avenue.

She stayed with me for four days. On the fifth day, I drove her back down the Avenue, waited while she packed, and drove her to the airport.

I didn't ask. She didn't say.

I had only driven a few blocks when the memory of the sun filtering through the shutters to glisten on her eyelashes and then move across the seductive flesh of her inconceivably perfect body covered the windshield and forced me to pull over.

Once at the Tate Gallery in London I went to view a Sir Lawrence Alma-Tadema Exhibit. A pillar of the Victorian Art world, his paintings were set in luxurious reconstructed Rome. The way he painted marble comes the closest to capturing the seductiveness of her skin.

Back at the apartment it seemed her scent had permeated every pore.

Along with the empty bottles, I trashed the sheets, towels, the two Brooks Brothers shirts she had worn, and a new tooth brush.

I opened every window.

Goddamn her!

I took another shower and put on a suit.

Goddamn her! Even in sex she was limited in passion.

I replugged the phone.

I'm finished with her.

Fuck her!

Deep down I knew I should be damning Stebo.

I ran down the steps and across the Avenue to catch the streetcar down to Carrebee's.

Shit. The pavement was steaming and it wasn't even noon.

57

"Son," Oliver said. We had passed the "Mr. Carrebee" stage. "Comes a time when even a thoroughbred needs to be put down."

"I'm sorry I didn't call, Oliver."

"No need to be. I knew where you both were. We were there. We were all there. Look here, Lizbeth Anne and I were planning to go to the Homestead Friday for a week. You know, up in Virginia. Well, she's feeling poorly so you go. It's all paid for. You go. Do you a world of good."

I went. I should have stayed. I returned to discover that the fiddler was finally going to be paid.

* * *

5

My seersucker suit was wilting and a river of sweat was running down my neck as I hurried to catch the St. Charles Avenue streetcar. The humidity level had to be over one hundred percent. I was late for work. I was late a lot. I was in the middle of my breakdown. Months before, Baby had impulsively jetted to Paris where she enrolled at the Cordon Bleu Institute where she would be awarded a medal as well as a diploma. I, just as impulsively, would succumb to an overpowering force and an even more overwhelming desire on the streetcar when life once again became "What's it all about, Alfie?"

Lipton's instant tea, fortified with Taaka vodka, started my day. (Did you know that Sir Thomas Lipton, founder of the tea empire and later confidant of Edward VII and yachting rival of the last Kaiser, began his career as a streetcar conductor in New Orleans? Well, he did.)

Anyway, I had this big knot in my stomach and a death wish in my head.

While most conductors will not stop for tourists because they hate them, they will wait for Uptown people to cross to the neutral ground if the streetcar is already at an authorized stop.

I don't blame conductors for hating tourists. They come to New Orleans in their proletariat caps, think they are going native by going practically naked, buy those awful T-shirts on Bourbon Street that read "Christ Is Coming and Boy Is He Pissed" or something really too obscene to repeat, stay drunk, and urinate in our streets. (Pontificating diverts the subject of my black thoughts.)

This particular morning the conductor applied his brakes and came to an abrupt halt directly opposite me while I waited for a break in the traffic to dash to the neutral ground about a block away from the legal stop.

"Thanks," I said on boarding. "Certainly appreciate your stopping. Besides my being late, it's too hot to run."

"No problem," he replied. "But, best go get a cool window seat before I let those people waiting at the stop on."

The streetcar is the second most fun thing one can do in the morning before arriving at one's office. There is always the familiar face of a friend or relative to be found. One can chat away about last night's party, who's having a breakdown, or who's going to be Queen of Carnival. Believe me, it's sublime. Even if there is no seat, conversations can be conducted by speaking over the heads of others. One can also wave to friends on the street or in cars, or better yet, flirt with pretty girls in convertibles who will blow one a kiss if one is "darlin'." Once Tal Peabody and I were going downtown and, at a red light, two proud beauties blew me a kiss. He asked me who they were and when I said I had no idea, he confided no one had ever blown him a kiss. At that time it was just about the saddest thing I had ever heard. Then, of course, strange things can and do happen on the streetcar, and one can learn things by observing.

One morning, for instance, the august King Calhoun got on. Despite the fact that his ego needed a cathedral to contain it, he, his wife Amanda, and their nine children lived in a rambling Tudor house in Old Metairie. So to see him leave the Carroll Apartments and board the streetcar was cause for consternation. I mean, the Calhouns considered themselves too grand for the Catholic church. A priest actually came to their house on Sunday to conduct a mass in their front hall. Also to be considered was the smile on his face and the jauntiness of his step. King was not a natural smiler; neither was Amanda, whose skin had the finish one usually associates with fine, hand-rubbed English saddles. Amanda excelled at sailing, skeet shooting, golf, tennis, riding, skiing, and birthing. Super jock that she was, all nine of her children were exceptional looking and tall. Not an ugly one in the litter.

"Mighty fine morning isn't it, Sudduth?" he greeted me. "Mind if I sit with you?"

King Calhoun was really happy that rainy, overcast morning. I had never seen this man really happy. Haughty, yes. Happy, no. I knew right then and there by his "mighty fine" greeting that King had a girlfriend. Or, as I once heard a Yankee salesman suggest to the saintly eighty-two-year-old president of G. A. Braun at a textile convention: "I could fix you up with a little something on the side tonight, Mr. Braun, if you'd be interested?" To which, Mr. Braun replied: "I admit it has been a long time, young man, but to the best of my knowledge it has not been moved."

Well, once a week became twice a week, became thrice a week. King just became happier and happier and about a year-and-a-half later he married his twenty-three-year-old secretary and became supremely happy. Forever I hope, after ALL the trouble he caused.

The St. Charles Avenue streetcar line is the world's oldest, running continuously since 1835 twenty-four hours a day, seven days a week. As late as the 1960s, the fare was only a dime, and today it is only sixty-five cents. Iconoclasts who denigrate the cars for lacking air conditioning and heating choose to forget that the windows open and close—in fact they are adjustable—and that one can raise or lower the canvas shades. The streetcar is our gallant legacy to the United States.

But back to the black streetcar conductor. Yes, he was a black man, about thirty years old with the whitest teeth I had ever seen, when I finally noticed them the day after my public breakdown began.

All I could see were moving lips and white teeth. I couldn't hear what they were saying for the roaring in my ears. I had fainted. First time in my life. I was epicly hungover. Rayne Farr and I had brawled at Forty-One/Forty-One, a singles bar she favored, and I think I had a concussion from being hit in the head with the ashtray she picked up after my nerves went haywire and the drink I threw in her face hit her like a tidal wave and with the same effect.

That morning I was the only person at the stop. It was still hot. Hotter than ever. Hotter than hell. The insides of my eyelids felt as if they had been sandblasted. Forgetting that someone might be trying to get off, I stepped up and was suddenly confronted by the hairiest and ugliest legs God ever put on a woman. The odor emanating from between them assaulted my nostrils about the same time the burned off nub of her arm brushed my mouth and hit me in the nose. The coup de grâce was the dried buttermilk on her heavy black moustache. It was enough to make even John Wayne give way.

Well, right there on St. Charles Avenue, Sudduth Meadows Spencer passed into unconsciousness in the dirt. I don't know how long I was out before I finally began to understand what he was saying:

"Jesus Lord, don't let him be dead. Are you dead, Mister? Mister, can you hear me? Jesus, Lord, don't be dead!"

I forced myself to say I was not dead, and he gave me the biggest smile I ever saw.

"You should be in toothpaste commercials," I muttered.

He laughed like hell.

"He ain't dead. You people give this fine white gentleman room to breathe," he ordered, and grabbed a newspaper from one of the peering people and began to fan me.

He became an integral part of my life after that. Most mornings he waited opposite my apartment as I scurried across the Avenue. All that summer I had a window seat on Streetcar 953. If he saw me on Canal Street during the afternoon, he would clang the bell, smile, and wave. In the evening, when the crowds on Carondelet can be brutal, with people pushing and jockeying for a position near where they think the streetcar will stop, he would open the doors only at the place where I was standing. These little blessings that can make life so pleasant and civilized I just accepted and took for granted.

When Geoff Badel, a half-generation Uptown transplant, whose father had made a fortune converting abandoned factories and warehouses to pseudo palaces of contrived conviviality, turned to me one morning and said: "That darky has an acute case of the hots for your aristocratic ass," my response was to yell, "You're crazy."

"Don't be so damn obtuse, Suddie," he shot back. "Surely you must realize his favored treatment of you transcends even your inbred sense of *noblesse privilége*. Do you really think it's right that he waits for you in the morning and stops the car in front of you in the evening?

After all, he is not your personal driver. Tell me, Sudduth, how many generations does it take to assume that God-given-right attitude you Uptown people have?"

"For someone who works for his father in somnolent ease, and then only between regattas and wenching, you talk like a sewer-mouthed Communist," I retorted.

"Touché, pride of Country Day!" he said.

We both laughed. Good humor restored, I promptly forgot the conversation.

* * *

6

Nothing is good when

the love of one's life is gone. Baby had been gone, forever. Perhaps she was only a half-fairy creature, but I loved her. And her substitute had nearly finished me off. Not that Baby could or should ever be compared with what came along. For whatever transpires between Baby and me, what's between us, will never die. After Paris, she became a transcontinental houseguest, so to speak. Friends reported seeing her *en passant* in Spain, London, Scotland, Newport, New York, Mexico ... even at Highlands.

"Looking lovelier than ever, but, God, is she drinking." In London she was chased by all five sons of the Marquis of Chandros. From the eldest, and heir, to the youngest.

"I loved them all," she told Mayday Martinay. "But their daddy was the best. Unfortunately, the divine man was born married. Also, their house doesn't have central heating and if I don't think of my weak lungs, who will? Anyway, Lamb, actually his name is Lambert, he's the oldest boy, and whoever he marries will be faced with living on the third floor when he inherits, because his daddy is to turn that really splendid old pile over to the National Trust. It was either that or sell. Pity, really."

In Mexico Baby captured the heart of a now-famous artist who was painting her when, on going into dinner, she insisted that he precede her.

"No, darlin', really," she insisted. "Ability before privilege." And she shocked and charmed a Catholic priest with, "Well, I certainly do believe in God and church on Sunday, but I also believe in hot sauce Monday through Saturday."

When overhearing a well-known pederast in Newport loudly berating his rather sad wife, Baby walked up to the man and said:

"I didn't know buggers could be choosers" and attempted to comfort the poor woman by reminding her that "while there's death, there's hope, honey."

A "pestering Yankee boy" finally heard, "NicholASS, if you really must know, I'd just as soon sit in a room and watch the wallpaper peel," and justified herself with, "Well, he wouldn't leave me alone. So I treated him just like a mosquito."

And at Highlands, Baby decided to take up golf.

"Don't you love it," she would tell people. "Who would have thought it?"

Gone. Gone so very long. I would have sold my soul for even a postcard from her.

One melancholy evening as I stared blankly out the streetcar window, an Annie Hall incarnate threw herself in the seat next to me, opened her bag, pulled out a banana, peeled it half way down, and salaciously began to lick it. I was mesmerized. I had never seen anyone lick a banana to death. I kept waiting for her to take a bite.

She had pouty lips and a talented tongue that was without doubt truly beautiful. Until that moment I had never been into tongues. Suddenly she turned and asked if I wanted a lick or a bite.

"I just love bananas and big organs. Church organs, that is," she purred.

(She really did like church organs, too.)

Common sense told me to pull the cord and get off the streetcar right then and there, but I already had an erection. My first real one since Baby departed.

God! She was like a purring puma.

"Ah. . . . No thank you. My name is . . . "

"White boy, I know your name. It's in the paper enough. Usually with Baby Soniat or some other debutante. How is Baby?"

"Baby is away," I struggled to say.

"Silly, I mean how is Baby. Bet I'm better. Know I'm better. Nobody does it better."

"I bet," I said, "but you mustn't talk about Baby and don't call me white boy." I could tell by her cocktail eyes she didn't like that. "Listen, today's Wednesday. Let's get off at Que Sera. You'll like it. How come I've never seen you there? What's your name?"

"Rayne R–A–Y–N–E Farr."

Que Sera, on St. Charles Avenue, is the place to be on Wednesday. From four to seven, a trio of drinks in plastic cups can be had for $1.75. By six, tables, portable bars, and much-pleasured people have inundated the sidewalk and neutral ground. It's our own little weekly Mardi Gras.

"Preppy, I don't do Que Sera. That's High School Harry and Joe College. I fuck. You like to fuck?"

"Yeah. I sure do."

"I'll tell you right now, I'm not one of your Uptown debs. I'm from across the river and I won't call you Suddie. 'Suddie' and 'Baby' is worse than 'Jack' and 'Jill.' Talk about being too-o-o precious. Yuck!"

I was throbbing and my pressed testicles ached. It was like my first time in the whorehouse off Rampart Street when I was seventeen.

Geoff Badel introduced me to Miss Effie's two days after I was graduated from Country Day. Geoff's swarthy Cajun looks and Grand Canyon deep cleft chin have been catnip to women since he was eleven-and-a-half years old. That's no lie, either. That was his age when he was caught with one of his parents' maids, Sally. She was in her twenties and he "gave her a baby," as they used to say. His parents gave her lots of money, and Sally and Baby Geoffery moved to Houston. He was also caught with Landry Pope when she had her breakdown during her parents' messy divorce when we were in

Middle School. After that, he was never caught again.

"I can read you like a book, Spencer. Here, throw this banana out the window. I've got your attention. I live on General Pershing. Four houses from that Clubhouse that keeps your kind so rarefied. I've made Uptown." And literally she would, too. The way Grant took Richmond.

"By the way I'm not a whore. Just better. Actually, I'm in real estate. Commercial properties, though. Like...."

"Honey, you could sell me the Whitney Bank Building downtown any day of the week." I felt good. Real good.

"Trust you to say the Whitney Bank," she remarked.

"What?"

"Nothing. You still want to come?"

"Damn right I do!" I said with unadulterated sincerity. She was a special breed and I wanted nothing more than to breed.

My alacrity made her laugh, and her eyelashes licked lightly at her high cheekbones. She started untying my bow tie.

"Hey, what the hell are you doing?" I brushed her hands away.

"This, white boy," and with that she ripped the tie from under my collar and threw it out the window.

"That was one of my favorite ties, you're crazy." I was peeved.

"I've been wanting to do that for a long time. Go back for it, white boy, and you can't come. Come on, you know you love it."

I did too. "White boy" really turned me on.

Accomplished in every sensual art, she was the most evil, most demented woman ever allowed to live. She could do things to a man's body that could make a bass baritone's voice shrill so high that only bats could hear it and so low that stallions would rear upon their hind legs. She went through me like a swamp fire. She was like a beautiful venomous snake and definitely of the jackal persuasion. Sex was not her consuming passion. Jealousy of what she wasn't part of was. Except for the sex fits, I treasure every moment I do not see her.

Rayne Farr actually disliked me. She told me so. Until that particular dusky evening at Forty-One/Forty-One, I had only known people who were predisposed toward me. Personal odium was something I had never experienced. Even today, a rebuff can still surprise me.

"Must you always be sarcastic?" I had rejoined to her mocking jab at my new jacket.

I was wearing a russet raw silk jacket I had seen at Brooks Brothers while buying shirts. Their Italian tailor, Gino De Cesare, had spent untold time over three fittings. I mean this jacket, besides being handsome, was flawless. I had been complimented about fifty times that day already, from strangers as well as from friends at Hollingsworth and Hart, where I had gone at lunch to pick up some collars that were ready.

"Trust you to wear the sign of the slaughtered lamb," she snarled as I leaned down to kiss her.

So much for feeling super.

"What are you talking about?" I asked.

"Your buttons, white boy. The 'Brothers' Brook' emblem always reminds me of a slaughtered lamb," she replied loathingly.

"Two-thirds of the time, Rayne, you act as if you don't like me. Why?" I matter-of-factly inquired while ordering drinks.

"I don't, preppy."

"You don't like me?" I felt dead.

"That's right, 'Suddie.' I really can't stand you."

"But you sleep with me. Pursued me."

"So what!" she retaliated. "I didn't like you. I wanted to deflate your pompous head."

"I am not pompous!"

"Oh yes you are! That's what's so maddening about you. You don't even know it. You honestly think God exists in his heaven just for you."

"You never liked me, once?" I couldn't believe her.

"Not much. Sometimes I did. One time I missed you."

"When was that?" I was very controlled.

"The time you were at that 'fine' dinner party for the new consul general of France. Remember? I called and the butler said everyone had just gone in and I told him to get you anyway because it was an emergency. The fool did it. Remember how I ripped your dinner clothes off in the living room? But most of the time you intimidate me."

"I 'intimidate' you? My feelings for you are ... always have been ... genuine. There's never been any rebounding involved." I was very controlled.

"So what! Your feelings for Baby are genuine, too."

"Don't talk about Baby, Rayne." I was very controlled.

"I'll talk about whom I damn well please, preppy. Especially the sacrosanct Baby! Why mustn't I? Because she doesn't do those 'not nice' things to your body? Hell, she'd do them to . . ."

That's when I threw the drink in her face and jumped up. My hands were choking her when she smashed the side of my head with the ashtray.

"If I had a gun, I'd kill you," she screamed as I fell back.

"Why bother? You already have," was all I said.

And so my public breakdown began. By morning, it was the talk of Uptown. I didn't regret what I had done, but I did so hate being told by a bartender that if I ever returned the police would be called. There is a certain indignity in being barred from a singles bar.

I was bad off after this. Nothing made me happy. Over the next month I lost about twenty pounds and had, for the second time, pneumonia. The first time I had pneumonia was when Rayne ripped off my clothes. It had been wonderful. I'll not deny that. We were on the floor, however, and her window air conditioner was blowing at gale force. I have weak lungs. So does Baby. The second time was the result of passing out at Galatoire's. I hadn't eaten in three days. Gala-toire's is usually kept at freezer room temperatures and being run down, well . . . I was passing out a lot and having visions. Sometimes I would see Rayne or Baby when they weren't there. Sometimes by the side of my bed. Sometimes when after-dinner coffee and brandy was being served in flower-filled rooms. When I saw them, I would tear and have to excuse myself. It was terrible. Joise, at Toy Cleaners on St. Charles, told me one morning, "Mr. Spencer, we're all so worried about you. I want you to know we're praying for you."

Joise Fuch is one of the sweetest women in New Orleans. Not only was she praying for me, she gave me these magic money beans. I forget by whom and where she has the lima beans blessed, but once they're blessed, they become money beans. It means one will always have money. When Joise gave them to me, I asked her if that meant I were going to be rich.

"Not necessarily, Mr. Spencer," she answered in that husky voice of hers. "But you'll never be poor. You'll always have enough money, which is a wonderful feeling."

And it's proven true. It really has. I always manage to have enough money. Unfortunately, sometimes people have died for me to get it.

When I moved to Washington, D.C. my office beans were lost. I keep some at the house and some at the office. I nearly had an anxiety attack. I called Joise, and in about a month she sent me four new ones. These I keep in a guarded place.

Joise also sends me cookies, even though I have now been gone over five years. She sends me boxes of Pepperidge Farm cookies. Joise doesn't cook anymore, you see.

While Joise and her co-workers were praying for me, my libido died. I really couldn't function. Johnny Lee's "Looking for Love in All the Wrong Places" and Patsy Cline's "Crazy" would set me off. These were songs associated with Rayne, and they were played in just about every bar where I sat morosely drinking. My blood may not have been in the gutter, but my guts certainly were.

That's how I met Cateland and Buckley Dennis. Actually, I met Buck first. I think Buck had been in the Moon Bar about a week when Cateland, his wife, found out where he was and came to take Buck home and, because Buck and I had now become boon companions, took me too.

As Cateland later told me:

"I just knew the condition of your soul was deplorable and my heart went out to you, honey. I knew who you were right away from your pictures being in the paper. But even if I hadn't, I would have taken you home. You needed help."

God really did send Cateland and Buck to me. This is the way I think. Rayne ridiculed my belief in God. Said my personal and child-like belief revolted her.

I am what I am and I'm not ashamed, either. I am a 1928 Prayer Book Episcopalian.

Well, we became fast friends. We still are. Cateland started fattening me up on good Southern cooking and REAL mashed potatoes. (Did you know that there are children today who have never had real mashed potatoes?) At Cateland's house I didn't drink. She and Buck were there through a bad time.

Eventually, I came to know and like all the members of both their families. Cateland's father was Dean at Nicholls State University in Thibodaux. That's Cajun country, about eighty miles west of New Orleans. Her father was also a deacon in the Baptist church. Buck's father was Thibodaux's best and most reputable mechanic. His mother was a registered nurse. His parents taught Sunday school at the same Baptist church. Buck must have been a throwback, for he certainly was the exact opposite of his quiet parents.

Buckley Dennis was called Buck by his father, Buckley by his mother (it had been Miss Faye's maiden name) and, since the age of fourteen, Tripod by the members of the basketball team of which he had been captain. The nickname produced a lasting swagger. Cateland called him Buckie. Lean, muscular, tall, and very good looking, Buck still wore the tight button-fly Levis of his youth with his cigarettes in the arm of his T-shirt, when he was not wearing his very worn black leather jacket, and his hair in a ducktail.

"Sudduth, you need a real sweet, loving, Christian girl," Cateland would cajole. "I've loved Buckie always, but deep down inside me since he was sixteen and I was thirteen years old and kinda plump. I was talking to my girlfriends on the school steps just before the last bell when Buckie roared up on his motorcycle that his precious mama saved up to buy him for his birthday, and I fainted just after he parked. I was just that overcome, you see. After that, I pledged myself to him and prayed fervently three times a day for him to marry me, and we married the day after I graduated from Daddy's school. I was a virgin," Cateland confided. "Honey, I can tell you that because I love you like my brother." I instinctively knew she could not have been otherwise.

The wedding albums were a testimony to the fact that their wedding had been the largest in the town's memory. Cateland had starved herself to Jacqueline Kennedy slenderness and Buck had forsaken his ducktail for an Ivy League haircut. The distinctive Kennedyish quality in the wedding portraits is especially evident in the pictures of them surrounded by well-wishers following the reception.

Cateland's going away dress was a peach linen sleeveless sheath with matching pill box hat, shoes, and bag. Her short white kid gloves evoked the style and elegance that proletarianism replaced. Buck wore a blue pinstripe suit with a white oxford button down collar shirt and English rep tie. They appeared to be running for public office. They honeymooned in New Orleans.

Buck bragged to me that on their first night together Cateland fainted. Later she had told him about the first time she fainted on the school steps when she saw him on his motorcycle, and how she now knew what had happened to her all those years ago.

Buck was the only genuine egoist I have ever known and, when drinking, stayed lost in a self-congratulatory reverie of his sexual prowess.

"Hell, Spence, my Babe was still reeling when she asked me if we could do it again."

"Really," I said. That was all that was needed.

"That's for real, my friend," he leered. "I told her, 'Yeah, Babe, we can do it again. We can do it all the time now.' "

Now Buck wasn't mean and he wasn't thick. Actually, he was bright. But he was trifling. He was also spoiled. Spoiled to death by his mama, by his women, and much-spoiled by his Cateland. He was Cateland's dream lover.

The "Big Easy" enthralled them, and almost immediately they decided they would return to spend the rest of their lives there together. Buck boasted that Cateland was glowing like a nuclear reactor before meltdown when they returned. "I swear to God, every one of her girlfriends was pea green with envy. Babe doesn't know this, but I was in even greater demand than before I married her. Let me tell you, there were mornings when I didn't think I could get it up. You know?"

"Yeah, I know." That was all that was needed.

They returned to New Orleans within a month and rented a furnished apartment at the very darned end of a silk stocking street in Uptown. This tragic queen of a house, crisscrossed with rusting fire escapes, was owned by an abortionist. To me, the six plastered brick Ionic pillars across its once-proud front always seemed to be weeping. Perhaps because the beau-

tiful cast-iron fence made by hand in Philadel-
phia had gaps like missing teeth. With its front
and back gardens cemented over, there was one
lone note of beauty, like the last camellia, a rose
bush that grew to the left of the front steps.
Buck planted the rose bush to commemorate
his first wedding anniversary after "I first took
an ax to that god-awful cement, Spencer. My
Babe cried for a week. For real, she was that
happy."

Neither had trouble finding jobs. Cateland
was welcomed by the Baptist Missionary Board.
Her major had been religion and she arrived
highly recommended. In time she was to head
fundraising for Overseas Missions. Buck went
to work for a rug company laying carpet since
the only thing he knew about cars was how to
wreck them. He certainly had inherited no ability or interest in mechanics from his father.

"Carpet seems fittin'," he would tell people.
"I'm good at laying things. Shoot, I'd lay a rattle-
snake if there wasn't any pussy around."

Cateland's flush would cover her freckles
and go to the roots of her dark hair, but she'd
hug him and kiss his cheek.

Cateland's days may have been spent spread-
ing the word of the Lord, but her nights were a
mad, teeth-gnashing concert of sighs and deeply
felt sounds. According to the neighbors I met,
they would have to bang on the walls or floor
to quiet the two of them down. They lived on
the first floor. Buck would preen, and likened
himself to an Olympic medalist swimming
against a strong current. Would Cateland have

preferred a terse tattoo of muffled love calls? Who knows? But their nightly mating established his reputation.

Cateland was very much like the woman who washed and ironed for Mother. Mattie was her name, and every Saturday her husband would take her money, get liquored up, and, come Sunday morning, slap her around. Most Mondays she would be in terrible shape. Mother, who had "listened" beyond the call of duty and kindness for years, one morning told Mattie she must leave him, and offered to find, and even pay for, a lawyer.

"I knows I should. I knows you're right. But Miss 'Bella, I sure do love my Friday nights."

Every night was Friday night for Cateland. Cateland had been born "little Mary Sunshine," but marriage made her delirious. Not even four miscarriages in a row lowered her spirits. Cateland never had a bad day. It was amazing!

About a month after Cateland's final miscarriage, Buck came down with mumps. Inflammation of the testicles left him sterile. When he was well, he took to heavier drinking, and later nights.

"Sudduth, I told him, honey, don't be depressed, I don't need children. I don't need anybody but you. If we had a hundred babies, I'd still love you best."

I think in time his sorrow might have passed, but in six months he had tuberculosis. Mumps were one thing, but tuberculosis made him feel unmanly. Buck firmly believed only women had tuberculosis. Perhaps he and Cateland had sat

81

through too many viewings of Greta Garbo in *Camille* at the Prytania Art Theatre. Cateland and Buck loved the movies. We used to go all the time to the dollar nights.

Well, Buck's recovery was long. So long he never returned to work. He is still recovering. The splendid teeth and princely features that attracted a thousand women have paid the price of being a legend, even if a secondary one. However, Buck's still whippet thin and certain kinds of women still pursue his rakish charms. And Cateland? Cateland's still happy and, most of all, she still loves Buck with the same blind-to-all-faults devotion of her girlhood.

Last year they celebrated their silver wedding anniversary in the same furnished apartment. Cateland wrote that Buck took poker winnings and had silver letters attached to a necklace that spelled out "I always love you best." As I said, he is her dream lover and she doesn't want to dream alone.

Cateland and Buckley helped, but Oliver was still worried sick. He thought I'd end up like his sons. So he sent me to the same psychiatrist who had treated two of his sons and still treated Junior. Why Oliver had such faith in this doctor, I don't know. Lord knows his sons certainly weren't any shining testament to normalcy.

I went, but my advice to anyone who thinks they need a psychiatrist is: "Don't fool with a noncommunicative shrink." The good doctor wanted me to begin at the beginning, so I started with the streetcar and the girl with the banana.

He stopped me with, "No, Mr. Spencer, I mean begin in the womb."

"Doctor," I said as I turned around to look at him, "I see no need of my returning to the womb mainly because I don't think anyone could have memories of their first nine months. I also don't believe in Sigmund Freud. Anyway, I had a perfectly normal and happy childhood. I'm just sorry it ended."

"Mr. Spencer, no one had a normal childhood. But so be it."

"I'm sorry. But that is what I believe. Shall I leave?" I started to rise.

"No, stay. Please." His hand motioned to me to stay. "Already I know I've never met anyone like you."

"Well, sir, I do believe in those ink tests."

"Do you mean the Rorschach test, Mr. Spencer?"

"Yes, doctor, could we begin with them?"

I was politely informed that those tests were considered passé. In fact, he didn't believe in them and had never used them.

After that, he only spoke on two other occasions. The first time was when I asked him if he had ever attended a "Come As Your Fantasy" costume party at the Lawn Tennis Club.

I asked him that because I had invited some friends to lunch at the club who were not members and they were late. While waiting, I started studying the framed pictures of past parties hanging in the reception area. In one group picture was the homeliest woman I had ever seen, dressed as a practical nurse. She was so homely that she was pathetic. Then, like a kick-in-the-ass, I realized that was no woman, that was my psychiatrist, the good doctor, who looked exactly like a Levantine Ichabod Crane. So come Wednesday afternoon, I asked him about it because I knew he wasn't a member.

"Yes, it is I, Mr. Spencer. Does it shock you?" he said in his low voice.

"Not particularly. I just wondered," I answered blasély.

Actually, I was shocked as hell. I mean, Oliver is spending all this money on me and I'm telling this man my deepest inner thoughts and his fantasy is to be a homely practical nurse. It did something to me. Really.

I thought about telling the doctor about my reclusive great-uncle Livingston, reputed to be the most exacting person who ever lived. Except for his cook, and an old man who tended the flower and vegetable gardens and did odd jobs, Livingston had been secluded in an American Gothic brown frame house way out in the country for untold years. The person closest to him was my grandmother, his sister, who visited him about once a month. Sometimes I would be taken to keep her company. I never went willingly.

Uncle Livingston's cook kept her head shaved. This woman, I forget her name, had an amazing collection of wigs. One blonde one was of truly metallic brilliance, and she would pop it on the moment I arrived with Nana. She was crazy for my blond hair and once asked to snip a piece off so she could order a wig of the same color.

His gardener/odd-job man was a demented old tartar. How he ended up in Louisiana no one knew or cared to ask. Probably because of his eyes. They were like flames. Burning flames. Really. He hated Nana. When she passed him or when her back was turned, he would spit with much contempt. Kahn, that was his name, never forgave Nana for commenting that the much-tended asparagus, used in the buttered asparagus rolls she favored, was "perhaps, just slightly tough this year."

The last time I was ever there we stayed for dinner. When my plate was placed in front of me, I asked Uncle Livingston's cook to please remove the fat from the pork chops. As a child I refused to eat anything that was rimmed with fat. Well, this nice-looking man with the cruel mouth just exploded. I was informed that it was not my place to order his cook about. My parents were obviously remiss and lax in attending to the duty of my training. My manners were appalling. I would eat the pork chops or eat nothing. If I ate nothing, he would personally thrash me with his crop. Nana couldn't even reason with, much less placate, him.

"Livingston, he's just a child," she protested. "Let it be, please. You're spoiling the memory of our day together."

"That child is a guest in my house. How dare he order my cook," he continued to shout.

So we left. When the Senator found out, he wrote Uncle Livingston a letter because there was no phone in the brown house in the country. I don't know what the letter contained. As far as I know though, neither man ever spoke to or saw the other again. In fact, the Senator refused to attend the man's funeral when he died about seven years later.

When I was moving to my first apartment where I would begin recreating the ambience of my grandparents' Edwardian elegance, I was in the attic going through trunks and boxes. I'm very fond of attics. Mother was giving me lots of furniture and things, but the best things were in the attic. That was also what I found so appealing about Carrebee Publishing Company.

Anyway, in one trunk was an ivory box containing at least two to three dozen photographs of this really lovely woman dressed in the most exquisite costumes. From Cleopatra to French Can Can dancers. From Marie Antoinette to a bewitching geisha. All these pictures had been taken in a vaguely familiar room over a number of years, for the woman, while still beautiful, aged. I brought them downstairs along with other things for the apartment and that evening, when Mother and I were having drinks, I opened the box and asked,

"Mother, who is this beautiful woman?"

"What, Sudduth?" She was thinking about Papa.

"I said, "Who's this beautiful woman, Mama?"

"What beautiful woman?"

"The woman in these pictures."

I handed them to her.

She looked at them and after a while answered.

"This beautiful woman is your great-uncle Livingston. He loved and lived for Halloween. He would always dress up for the trick or treaters. It was very sad. Living way out there, no children ever came."

Lucky children, I thought.

"And he went to so much trouble for them," Mother continued. "Why, he would order his costumes from New York and sometimes even from France. Only his cook ever really saw him. After she died, he had nobody to take his picture. Really, it was too sad. No one would believe how that lonely handsome man just lived for Halloween. He was astonishing as Flora, the goddess of flowers. He wore real flowers everywhere. I wonder where that one is. That was the last time I ever went. After that I wanted to be with my friends. Mama said I was selfish. These must have been in one of Mama's trunks. Things certainly can accumulate."

With that she tore the pictures up and threw them in the fire.

My doctor's soporiferous voice was heard for the next and last time, when he requested I not come back because I was "hopeless."

"A hopeless what?" I asked.

The good doctor never said.

Actually, I didn't need a psychiatrist to tell me Rayne Farr was a case study in dementia praecox. What I needed was someone or something to make the pain in my head stop and the knot in my stomach go away.

Any normal person would have been aghast at learning Rayne had aspired to sainthood as a nun. Academically, at St. Mary's Dominican College, she had done very well and was piously religious, especially come Sunday. Nevertheless, Rayne had twice failed the psychological tests that are required to determine if one is suited for a religious order.

Hell, I could have told the nuns at Dominican that, even before the bird incident. We were walking back to my car along the lower end of Canal Street where these god-awful office towers were put up in the flight path of birds. Every morning there are dead birds on the sidewalk. Well, I heard this heart-tearing shriek and before I could even look up, this bird bounced off me and landed at my feet.

"My God, that poor bird," I said to her.

"Step on it. You'll do it a favor," she said without any feeling or concern.

"For someone who aspired to be a nun, your lack of compassion is extraordinary, Rayne."

She became very silent and then asked me:

"What do you intend to do with the 'poor' bird?"

"We'll take her to Mother's vet and then I'll take you home."

"You can take me home now! I don't feel like sleeping with St. Francis of Assisi. It's a real turn-off, believe me."

I took her home. The bird recovered. In fact, the day the bird was diagnosed as well enough to rejoin its kind, Rayne called to ask if she could come spend the night.

She rang off with "See you in a hour, white boy."

When I opened the door she was naked, her raincoat around her ankles.

I knew I shouldn't have taken her to the new members' reception at The Round Table Club, but she had been pestering me to see the great white mansion, with the towering azaleas and wide veranda, across the Avenue from Tulane and Loyola and next to the entrance to Audubon Park.

The club had been founded by Dr. Beverly Warner, the pastor of Trinity Episcopal Church, back in 1898 when he met with a group of friends "to consider the formation of a club for literary, scientific, artistic, and learned gentlemen."

The illustrious symbol of the club is a half-size reproduction of King Arthur's legendary round table. The table was shaped by English craftsmen using two-inch thicknesses of quartered oak, and according to the club literature, decorated and lettered just like the original, except our colors are brighter and our names are easier to read. Another of our cherished traditions, along with Camelot night, is the celebration of William Shakespeare's birth.

Drinks were still being served on the veranda when Drake Monroe came up to tell me of Despanet de Blanc's death in the steam room at the New Orleans Athletic Club. Rayne and I were

89

surrounded by new and old members and she loudly blurted out:

"Sure bet his poor tired ass is glad."

"What?" I choked.

"Well," she flared. "He told me his life-long goal had been to do nothing but screw and sit on his ass."

"And just when would he have told you"....
Oh, God. I knew.

She looked at me defiantly.

Despanet de Blanc's family has cut me dead ever since that Saturday evening. I simply no longer exist to them.

Rayne excelled at inflicting stinging, long-lasting hurt. At this and sex fits, she could not be rivaled. Believe me, I know. The self-made president of the real estate company, where Rayne certainly seemed to be rising, and his wife were going to celebrate the two-year restoration of their Uptown house. The house had been built the year of the big yellow fever epidemic in 1897. Rayne insisted I attend. She was "proud of me." She wanted to "show me off." I was delighted and pleased to be shown off. Hadn't I long pleasured in being shown off? Going back to the days when Mack would take me to the Gethsemane Temple Church in my best white sailor suit from Best & Company in New York. True, sometimes I found being shown off tiresome. Once, at the country club, after enduring pats, kisses, and heaps of compliments directed at Papa and Mama regarding my precious looks and impeccable table manners, I picked up my empty ice cream dish and licked it clean. Mama still talks about that Sunday brunch.

Admittedly, our hosts may have been new to Uptown and to me, but I knew I could rise to the occasion and did. And they and their friends were graciousness itself. Our host didn't even flinch when Rayne dropped her drink on the handwoven rug designed for the library. His German wife had chic and style and tremendous energy, and her decorator had not been given carte blanche.

The evening had gone well. On saying goodnight, they thanked me for coming. Said I was charming. A perfectly delightful guest. Drop by anytime, with or without Rayne. He gave me a firm handshake and a pat on the back. She gave me a double-handed shake and a kiss on the cheek.

Rayne's jealousy destroyed the glow of the evening before we reached the front gate.

"You were a perfect shit in there. A perfect shit!"

"What in the hell are you talking about?" I was staggered. "They liked me. Everyone seemed to like me."

"God, what a preppy shit you are. You can get a taxi or walk home," she yelled.

We had come in her car. My car was getting new brakes.

"You're nuts! You know that? Nuts! Crazy! Leave me alone from now on! Understand?"

This happened on a Saturday night. Sunday, she rang. Asked if I would come for lunch after church. She never, I mean never, missed church. Never.

I forgot. Rayne also excelled at cooking. Lunch was Lucullan and it ended with the white grapes that she dipped in unbeaten egg whites and then rolled in sugar. She knew I loved them, and that afternoon she packed some in a plastic container for me to take. Even stuck a bow on the lid.

As I said, that was Sunday. On Thursday, we were at Forty-One/Forty-One. With Baby I had experienced chivalrous love. With Rayne, I experienced its degradation. I also learned that it's better to play with one's own kind.

* * *

7

Summer burned away and a hotter fall began. The asphalt was actually bubbling when I took an isolated bequest and impulsively joined my favorite second cousin for a month in Scotland. God knows I needed to get away.

This, my first unexpected legacy, showed me the power of Joise's money beans. (My money beans should not be confused with "gris gris," those Voodoo charms or amulets which I don't cotton to.)

My benefactor, the fine gentleman whom I honor on All Saints' Day still, had been a bachelor classmate of the Senator's. And, while I didn't remember ever meeting him, I had vague memories of having had fresh chipped beef for the first time with him and the Senator, and later of someone bringing me a large Mason jar of the same which made me sick because I ate so much.

In the lawyer's office I learned that he had

been seated at a nearby table at the country club the afternoon I picked up the empty ice cream bowl and licked it clean as an antidote to all that praise. This grandiose gesture on my part had charmed him no end. I had literally captured his heart, and he had been "observing" me ever since. So, the "handsomest and finest child ever born" was to receive some tax-free money. That the obviously pained and prurient attorney had looked out his office window the whole time he was telling me this didn't bother me in the least. To hell with him, I thought. He's just jealous.

I guess I had been back from Scotland about three days when I saw the black streetcar conductor for the first time in over a month. It was a Saturday morning. I was going downtown to Hollingsworth and Hart. Our favorite men's store was having one of its famous and private gambling sales. Benny, the presser, would be wearing white gloves, and mixing drinks from a bar set up near a craps table. The number of small black dots that turned up on the ivory cubes would determine the percentage of discount for each item bought.

I do not exaggerate. Hollingsworth and Hart is club-like. An exclusive club, that is. At one time the entire staff was composed of retired executives who wanted something to do for a few hours a day or sons of men who wanted something to do between sailing and cocktails. Many's the time I've heard "I don't believe we carry your size," said to one of the not-chosen by one man in particular at Hollingsworth and

Hart who could have intimidated God. Even I could become nervous around him, and that should tell you something right there.

Cooper had a way of peering over his half-moon spectacles that was awesome. Truly. Anyway, one autumnal Friday evening, just before closing time, I was lollygagging with Burt Kline. Burt and I are long-time friends. His grandson, Brian Berke, who was then a junior at the University of Colorado, had eclipsed Bubba Estes' wrestling wins the year before. Wins that had stood unchallenged for seventeen years. Bubba's finally ancient history after all these years. We stopped talking when Jason Charles charged through the front door weighted down with about five obviously new suits and an equal number of jackets.

Jason headed straight for Cooper and, without a by-your-leave, threw the clothes over the rack that holds all the country club trousers. That's what I call them anyway. You know what I mean. Madras. Pink and green patchwork. Solid yellow with red goldfish. Those types of trousers. This made me remember what the president of the firm that employed Rayne told me that night at his house. It shows how perceptive he was. As I said, he was self-made rich. He became rich because, in addition to being smart and aggressive, he understood things. What he said was this: "I can tell everything about a man by the way he dresses in his leisure. That's why I took up golf. Beats studying a portfolio every time."

Well, anyway, Jason, in his most imperious tone, told Cooper:

"My daddy says these clothes were poorly pressed. He wants them re-pressed, immediately."

Jason and I avoid each other. He knows I think he's a twit. I don't know what he thinks of me and don't give a damn because I know Jason can't think. He also looks exactly like Henry Fonda, whom I never could abide. Listen, the only person who ever had that much humility was crucified. Jason's father, Chase, I do like. He exudes bonhomie and nobody, I mean nobody, can lead a debutante across the floor the way Chase Charles can. There's something about his stride, carriage, and the way he does his arm and the angle of his wrist. It's something to see.

Cooper peered at Jason for a timeless moment before replying.

"Benny leaves at four on Friday. The steam has been off for two hours, and the store just closed. It's six o'clock. Tell your father his things will be ready Monday, at eleven."

"My daddy wants them now," Jason continued in the same tone.

"That's impossible."

"Do you know who my daddy is?"

Jason doesn't even have common sense, I think.

Cooper's voice was like a laser beam.

"Yes, I know who your 'daddy' is. Your father is Chase McDonald Charles. He came to New Orleans from Texarkana, Texas right out of college. He worked hard, married up, and made a lot of money. Your name is Jason Chase Charles, sometimes known as 'Little

Chase.' You went North to marry up. Tell your 'daddy' his things will be ready Wednesday, at eleven."

Jason, red-faced, turned and fled.

Come-uppance is just, especially when it comes to people who deserve it. Anyway, this is the way I think.

"Where you been," my friend, the conductor, asked as I boarded my favorite streetcar.

"I've been on vacation."

Did he look hurt? I quickly pushed the idea from my mind.

"Where to?" He was not smiling.

"Scotland."

"Scotland far away?"

"Yes," I said. "Very far away."

"Was it nice?"

"Very. Besides being blessedly cool, it's a land of lakes and mist. I see you've grown a beard," I said to change the subject. "You look like Edward VII."

"Who that?"

"He was the King of England a long time ago," I answered.

"Yeah?"

"Yeah."

"Was he black?"

"No. But you still look like him. A black Edward VII."

"You have a picture of him I could see?"

"No."

"I'd like to see this dude."

Later that same day I was at Smith's Drugstore. I had just finished my nectar soda and was charging two cartons of cigarettes and a half-gallon of Taaka vodka when I spotted a box of King Edward Cigars. I charged them too, for him.

Monday morning he was waiting for me. On boarding, I said, "Here's something for you."

"I don't smoke, but thanks."

A smile was starting to break across his face.

"I didn't know. Anyway, that doesn't matter. Look. See the fine colored picture of King Edward. You look just like him. You're a black King Edward."

"Well, I'll be, I sure do. Thanks. That's real nice. I've sure missed my fine white friend. I sure enough did."

"It's good to be home," I replied and went to sit by John-Boy Boyd in the last seat.

John-Boy is one of my best friends. Bonita-boo Boyd, his wife, is the ultimate charmer. Her infectious laughter and a carefree exterior disguise a very bright mind and even brighter business acumen. Bonita-boo plans parties in New Orleans for large Yankee corporations. When I'm with Bonita-boo and John Boy, I think of the magnitude of time and place. Actually, time and place can be as important as God, Grace, and Grandfather. Except for Baby, well....

Young and pretty as Bonita-boo is, she was born to be a dowager. When she throws her shoulders back, raises her chin, and says: "Ah know who ah am, thank God." Well, it's something to see.

The world needs more dowagers. My grandmother, Eva Elizabeth, was more royal than Queen Mary. One of her looks could turn a person to stone at ten feet and galvanize the most shiftless person to immediate action. Dowagers could have won the War. Any war. Believe me.

It was sometime after the cigars that my friendly "Good morning" was followed by his:

"Just looking at you makes me feel good all over."

I was so stunned all I could say was "thank you" and hurry to any seat far from the front.

How cavalierly I had dismissed Geoff Badel's heedings. Now I was faced with accepting the truth. Incipient bankruptcy and usurious open parking rates at the Superdome on Poydras Street precluded my even considering driving. Fuck the long walk both ways to Carrebee's and getting inside an oven-hot automobile in the evening.

I definitely had a problem. The cigars had been a Grand Military Fuck-Up. Those damn cigars had given him the chance to cross that thin white line. Not only was I thick, I was spoiled. I had been indulged too long. I liked having a window seat. I liked preferential treatment. I was accustomed to "preferential" then.

All that day I thought about my new problem. Another problem I did not need. I was engrossed in a manuscript about bonded fabrics when I realized how the intolerable situation could be rectified. I would buy an alarm clock. I have a marble and ormolu mantle shelf clock from my paternal great-grandparents that strikes on the hour and half hour, but I never owned an alarm clock. Normally I wake unaided.

All my life I have awakened to the whistles of the steamboats on the Mississippi. Their mournful sound, so romantic to tourists, has always reminded me of a death knell. Sometimes I think those morning, noon, and night high-pitched cries made us all neurasthenic as adults. It was either that or something in the water.

That evening I went to the K&B Drugstore on the corner of St. Charles and Napoleon and bought a Big Ben that was now made in Japan. When I was growing up, K&B was Katz and Bestoff but, like everything else, it has been initialized for people who can't read.

Come the next morning, I was at the legal stop waiting for an earlier streetcar, which must have been ahead of schedule, for after about fifteen minutes Streetcar 953 pulled to a stop, the doors opened and his voice yelled out to people I knew and people from nowhere:

"You trash get out of the way for this fine white gentleman. Get yourself on here, my friend. Why you walk way down here? You know I wait for you. I've been waiting for you a long time, a real long time."

To my horror, they did make room. I could only look at the design on the toes of my black wingtips as I stepped up and walked to the sound of Geoff Badel's laughter.

"Shut up. You hear me, Geoff? Shut up or I swear to God I'll tell everybody you're sleeping with your father's girlfriend and Samantha's twin sister."

"Suddie, I can't, I'm sorry, but I'll do the next best thing," he choked. He had laughed so hard that tears were running down from his red-rimmed eyes.

The next best thing was to get off the streetcar, which he duly did.

So much for Big Ben alarm clocks and my attempt to relinquish my assured seat.

I was still reading that bonded fabric manuscript, which had nothing to do with bondage, though it would have been a heap more interesting, when another solution presented itself. I would compromise. In the evening I would catch a later streetcar or, if pressed, call United Cab's private number to get Uptown in a hurry. There would also be no more staring at the toes of my shoes.

Feeling ever so relieved, I rang Mayday Martinay and invited her to go with me to Tipitina's. Mayday is deliciously muzzy and ever so relaxing. Just like a tonic. There are very few relaxing women left. It's a great pity. A man needs a relaxing woman at times. Mayday loves the Neville Brothers as much as I, and they were back home from a successful tour. Their music tells you to move your body to each drum beat and cowbell. Their music makes you walk like you hear music playing. Their music may be hazardous to your health, but if you're having a good time, it's what it's all about, Alfie.

Well, their home place is Tipitina's on Napoleon at Tchoupitoulas not far from the river. For

101

trashing out, there is nowhere finer. Not even in Carolina. Tipitina's is the best music place in the country, as well as the best party place.

Mayday and Baby loved Tip's, but Baby loved its Cajun food and Cajun music better. Most of all, Baby loved to go there to trash out with me or some other "lucky devil" and dance the blues away.

I took Baby there the night she was between adulations. The three men, whom Gay Noe McLendon had invited from Palm Beach to attend her annual "fais-do-do," at Baby's urging, one of whom was the polo player James Warren Nichols, no longer amused Baby.

Gay's fais-do-do was still being talked about. A fais-do-do is a Cajun hoe-down. Lots of dancing and, to go with all that dancing, Gay had served mountains of jambalaya, gumbo, red beans and rice, and crawfish étoufee. The party lasted till a sun-breaking Sunday morning.

Gay is the ultimate hostess. At her galleried Prytania Street mansion, she'll even invite tourists who are standing outside her gate taking pictures to come in for champagne. Her house has the city's largest ballroom. Her daddy was James A. Noe, former Governor of Louisiana, oil man, and radio/television mogul. Gay herself was married to Gordon McLendon, who was one of the richest men in the United States, according to *Forbes* magazine. He originated radio's "Top 40" format.

But Baby was missing Stebo this particular night. All systems on go. Every signal sign fully lighted. I knew them all. I'd certainly read them enough. Baby's drastic mood swings from sweetness to prime bitch, from quiet to loud, from ice maiden to teasing whore. Soon there would be a smash-up, another fight, tears on her part and drink on mine. When the band broke for intermission, I had decided win, lose, or draw to take her home.

"Let's go home, darlin', it's late. I'm tired. You're tired. We won't be able to move tomorrow, much less play tennis. How about it? An early night for both of us?"

"Are you manipulating me, Suddie?" she slightly slurred.

"You're unmanipulatable, Baby. I just want some good sets tomorrow. That's all."

"Well, then, you may take me home," she replied with infuriating largess. "I'm in your hands master. . . . what's that look mean, Sudduth Meadows Spencer?"

"What look?"

"That look you have on your face now. You've never looked that way at me before. What's come over you?"

"I was just thinking of all the good a good thrashing with a buggy whip would do you."

"Honey," she laughed. "You'd never harm a hair on this beautiful head, much less cut the skin on this body you worship."

"Let's go, Baby. I mean it. I'm not fooling."

We were walking to my car when a young black teenager yelling "Miss Soniat!" "Miss Soniat!" came running from across the wide avenue and stopped in front of us panting.

Baby stared blankly at him.

"It's me, Miss Soniat, Tommy. How you be? Sure good to see you."

"Fuck off, kid," Baby snarled.

Tommy's beaming face fell.

"Baby, for Christ's sake! Don't be such a...."
I wanted to rip her tongue out.

"Oh, honey, I'm sorry. Of course, I remember you. You're Rita's boy, Tommy. Tommy Sweet. Your mama taught me how to make her famous bread pudding when I used to stay with my Aunt Valkyrie. Rita always brought you to work with her except that awful day of the gas leak. Otherwise, you would have . . . 'My sweet Tommy' I called you. You used to sit in my lap then, and I would read to you from the book of fairy tales my daddy gave me when I was a little girl. You just loved the pretty pictures. Remember, you got so excited one time you wet your pants and my favorite pink dress from Marjorie's Morningstar. I forgave you because you were 'my sweet Tommy.' I'm sorry I used that awful word. It's just that I was missing my daddy and I've had too much to drink."

"It's OK, Miss Soniat. Hey, I knows you liked me. Mama, she used to say you spoiled me bad. Did you know some man shot my daddy dead last year? He was a night watchman. I'm living with my auntie now and working at Schwegmann's. I had to drop out of school."

"Do you work on Sundays?" Baby asked him.

"No, ma'm, Miss Soniat."

"Tommy," Baby said. "This is Mr. Spencer. We've known each other all our lives."

"Evening, Tommy," I replied, smiling at him. We shook hands.

"Mr. Spencer and I were going to play tennis tomorrow, but I want you all to be my guests at Galatoire's instead. You all will be my guests? Won't you?"

Baby said this in the voice that will get her into heaven. I could hear her at the Pearly Gates asking Saint Peter:

"Well, you are going to let me in, aren't you? I've only been a little bad."

"Of course," I answered, taking her hand and forgetting that just moments before I had wanted to rip out her tongue.

"Tommy?"

"Yes, ma'm, Miss Soniat. What time? My church, it be out at eleven-thirty."

"Do you know where Galatoire's is, Tommy?"

"Yes, ma'm. It's on Bourbon Street. Peoples, they always be lined up out front."

"Well, you meet us there around one. Don't stand in that awful line. Walk inside and tell Mr. André, he's the man at the door, you're my guest. Tell him I want him to take you to my table and bring you all the bread pudding and sauce you want if Mr. Spencer and I are late. See there, I even remember how much you liked the bread pudding I sometimes made."

Tommy grinned broadly.

"You always late, Miss Soniat. I remembers. I sure do."

"Well, honey, it's still true. I'm even worse now, but I really will try not to keep you waiting. I shall also call this friend of mine at the Whitney.

105

My friend may know something about 'stay-in-school' programs. I just can't bear the thought of you working at Schwegmann's. Langenstein's Groceries, at least, would have been social. Why, the area around Schwegmann's is terrible. After all, you were 'my sweet Tommy.' You are still sweet aren't you, Tommy?"

"I'm a good boy still, Miss Soniat," Tommy earnestly replied. "Maybe not sweet, because sweet, that was a long time ago. But I'm a good boy. Yes, ma'm, I am."

And so it came to pass that Baby did call her friend and Tommy was to return to school and later be graduated, with honors, from the University of New Orleans. Today, Thomas Sweet is a loan officer for the Whitney. He has a wife and two children. His son's name is Stebo Soniat Sweet. His daughter's name is Baby Soniat Sweet.

"Don't you love it," Baby would tell people. "Daddy and I will live on for at least another generation, and that's thirty years."

That night on Napoleon Avenue was actually Baby's finest hour, although she would disagree with me.

Baby, to this day, still maintains "My most shining hour was the Zoo-to-do. That was the year I became the first Double Queen ever."

It may have been her "most shining hour," but it was also her saddest. I know. I am the only one who knows. I was there. I took her.

May in New Orleans means only one thing— "Zoo-to-do," hosted by the Board members of the Audubon Zoological Gardens in Audubon Park for the patrons who have made our zoo the finest in the world. Walls, bars, and dismal cages have been banished. Fifty-eight acres of lush tropical vegetation, waterfalls, and century-old oaks that General "Beast" Butler would have used for kindling if the weather hadn't changed during Yankee occupation, permit animals to live contentedly in natural surroundings, while a network of moats and unobtrusive barriers make it possible for one to walk among them.

On that night the weather is always splendid. The best restaurants vie to set up booths that will cater to our love affair with food, zoo staff bring out animals to be petted and adopted, champagne corks explode, René plays, and the good times roll.

And this May night was the best ever. It was God-like. Every star shimmered its flickering glow on Baby's beauty. A low chanting chorus greeted her arrival. As soon as René saw Baby, he stopped the orchestra and switched to "If Ever I Cease To Love." The current Queen of Carnival, an unpopular legacy, thought René was honoring her. But those who knew, knew of René's devotion to Baby, and there was no question which queen was being honored when he motioned for Baby to join him on the stage at its conclusion.

"Go on, darlin', René's waiting," I said, releasing her hand and kissing her.

"Aren't you coming, Suddie?"

"No, honey. They want you. Not me."

As Baby approached the raised platform,

The Meters came on stage and, before singing the beloved Zoo-to-do song, dedicated "They All Asked For You" to Baby, who blew them a kiss.

The first stanza went like this, with "Baby" substituted for "you."

> *I went down to the Audubon Zoo,*
> *and they all asked for Baby.*
> *Yes, they all asked for Baby.*
> *They all asked for Baby,*
> *they even inquired about Baby.*
> *The monkeys asked, the tigers asked,*
> *and the chimpanzees, they asked too.*

Over a thousand guests were screaming, "Baby." René had his arm around her waist and Baby was waving and blowing kisses, but it was at the song's conclusion that pandemonium broke out. The orchestra switched to "Dixie," and Rebel yells cut through the night air. Napkins and handkerchiefs were waving and flowers ripped from bushes or centerpieces were being thrown at Baby's feet.

Had any real queen ever had such adulation? I realized Baby didn't need a husband. She needed a consort.

"Dixie" was still being played and flowers thrown when Baby kissed René, curtsied to her public, and returned to me.

"Suddie, please take me home. I'm sick. Very sick."

Smiling and gracious, we made our way through a crowd that parted like the Red Sea for us. In the car, away from everyone, Baby cried. Only once before had she cried like this. When Stebo died. I sat there holding her. Saying nothing.

"Don't you even want to know why I'm crying?" she asked sullenly, as she pulled away.

"I know why, Baby."

"You know?"

"Yes. You learned tonight what I learned in graduate school and why I left. It wasn't just the money. There are no second acts, darlin'. You're worried about what you'll do for an encore. Well, there won't be one, darlin'. Not you or anyone will ever top tonight."

"But, Suddie, I'm not even twenty-one. It's not fair."

"What about those who never have glory?"

"Oh, hush up. Don't you go being moral on me. And I certainly don't give a damn about those others. It's still not fair. Let's go back, then. If what you said is true, I might as well go back and enjoy every moment. Besides, I didn't even get any champagne or any of that divine food."

Anyway, Mayday Martinay and I had a super, if not too "relaxing" on my part, time at Tip's. Mayday is not like other former queens. She hasn't changed. Come the next morning when I boarded the streetcar, the hair of the dog was with me, but I had a clipped and cool "good morning" for the conductor's "My, don't you look fine today." With my head up, I stared down any embryonic snickers, walked to the last window seat, sat down, pulled from my briefcase that damned manuscript, and finally finished it.

It was grim in the evening. Humanity is crushing. I never had a seat. But even grimmer was the fact that I didn't seem to know anyone on the later streetcar.

My intrepid effort of the soul to keep him distant didn't succeed very well. The more sang-froid I became, the more favorably disposed he became, almost like a stray that wants to follow one home. I had no desire to take him home, but I certainly pleasured in having a seat most mornings.

So this is the way we continued. Continued through the first Tulane game, Halloween, All Saints' Day, Thanksgiving, Christmas, New Year's. Continued until the first big cold. And contrary to popular opinion, a New Orleans winter can be cold. Short, but cold. No snow. However, the ice and frigid temperatures can be awesome. When pipes freeze and burst, the threat of a conflagration makes everyone nervous because the city, especially Uptown, is constructed of wood, cypress mostly.

Well, on this particular glaciated Thursday morning there wasn't even water to wash one's hands, much less flush a commode. Rain began around eleven. Soon cars were careening into one another or any other non-moving object. Just before noon, the bridges were closed and the mayor shut down the city. I was one of the many who had braved to go downtown. Rain had not been forecast. Now I was sorry. People who had driven would either have to walk or take to the streetcars, and there were already reports of snapping lines in some sections. The wind-and-rain-mixed, pelting ice bit the face like buckshot.

Rumors were that lines on Canal Street were down, so I cut across to a stop opposite Lafayette Park. People were pushing and cursing and jam-packed streetcars were flying by. It was surreal. The exodus from Berlin as the Red Army advanced on the Brandenburg Gate.

Before being totally engulfed by the throng, I decided to walk and broke away. I had only walked a few feet when I heard what I knew must be Number 953 clanking its way down the Avenue. I turned. I was right. It was crowded to capacity, but it came to a screeching stop in front of me. A sea of people encircled me and began beating on the double doors. He must have opened them manually, for the next thing I knew he was on the steps bellowing as if he were a bear prematurely awakened from hibernation.

"You trash, I ain't got room but for one. This one." And he reached out and pulled me on, kicking out at faceless people.

"Give this fine white gentleman room! You hear me? Move it!" he ordered.

I didn't care.

The freeze was over by Saturday afternoon. Other than the replacing of untold miles of burst pipes and hundreds of palm trees, the city returned to normal. Burst pipes are not to be taken lightly. It is not uncommon for people to go for weeks without water. ANY water. Think about that. Percy Sue Hyams, who has several rental properties, was faced with replacing over eighty miles of pipe, including her own. To pay the plumber, she sold a house. Percy Sue also had bottled water hauled to her tenants.

Monday came and, to my wonder, Streetcar 953 passed me by. What the hell, I thought. Then I realized there was a different conductor. The next day, the following morning, and the next week, and the week after, he was gone. Where was he? Where had he disappeared to? The seat was unimportant. I became concerned. Had something bad happened to him? I missed him, too. Missed his smiling, happy face.

I called the transit office and asked to speak to the head of personnel. Her first question was:

"What is his name?"

"I have no idea, but he's the conductor on Number 953."

"I need a name, sir," she was impatient.

"Well, tell me this," I continued. "Has any conductor died or been murdered in the last three weeks?"

"No. Maybe he retired, sir. We've had two recent retirements."

"No. He's too young. He looks like a black.... Never mind."

"I'm sorry I can't be of more help. You must be a nice man. Most conductors are invisible to passengers."

"Thank you anyway," I said. "Goodbye."

Months passed. And everyday I looked for him.

* * *

8

I was Love-In-Idleness and trying to find my former self when I met this pretty Yankee artist and thought we could escape into the sins of Egypt.

I had dragged myself to Smith's Drugstore for breakfast. My head felt as if I had been beaten with a baseball bat. It was four in the afternoon. Next door to the Pontchartrain Hotel, Smith's is the best drugstore in the whole world. What other drugstore still delivers and will deliver pills, cigarettes, and vodka? And up to eight o'clock, too. Anyway, I was dying on the counter and Hildreth was cooking me breakfast. Three eggs over light, two rashers of bacon, and whole wheat toast. She knew I was bad off, so she was being very quiet. Hildreth's been in New Orleans long enough to have acquired its liberal attitude toward human frailties. Usually we talk about Germany. Next to England, I love Germany. Face it, the Royal Family's German.

Hildreth came to New Orleans as a German

war bride. She must have been a stunner. She's still pretty in a tired, worn way. I know she married down, and it's not based on a comment she made about military uniforms fooling people. I just know. She never complains, though, and I like her. Her dream had been to one day have her own business, and when that day finally came I was floored.

"You're leaving Smith's to open an upholstery shop," I repeated.

"Yes, Mr. Spencer, today is my last day. I've trained the new girl and told her to take care of you. But, yes, this is my last day. I know upholstery. My father had a fine business in Nuremberg. He taught me much. He had no sons. Just me, Hildreth. I was to inherit. We had a comfortable life. Mama had a cook and cleaning woman twice a week. We had a car. But the war came and took Mama, Papa, everything. But, ya. This has been my dream. Now, with Ed's insurance money, it is to be."

"Well, Hildreth, I plan to be your first customer. Don't cry. I mean it."

I really was her first customer, too. With great skill, Hildreth redid two 1850 footstools that I rescued from disgrace in the attic. Today, if I didn't know her, I couldn't afford her.

But all this was still to come, and right now Hildreth was cooking me breakfast.

"Sure smells good, Hildreth," I said to her. I was trying to rise to the occasion.

"You say that all the time, Mr. Spencer. You should learn to cook." Hildreth was smiling.

"You willing to teach me?"

"Shame on you, Mr. Spencer. Here I am a happily married woman with. . . . "

"I'll teach you," said a voice to my left.

I turned and three stools from me was this pretty, titian-haired girl about twenty-five.

"Teach me what?" I asked her.

Hildreth was really smiling now.

"Teach you to cook eggs the way she does," she replied, looking directly into my eyes.

"I was only teasing. Lord, we must support this soda fountain. It's just about the last one in the city."

"Well, I'm not teasing, I'll teach you to cook eggs just like hers, if you'll let me draw your hand."

"My hand?"

The toast was burning. Hildreth was transfixed.

"You want to draw my hand? Why?" Can't I ever meet anyone just reasonably normal, I thought.

"I'm an artist. I work for Saks. I came down from Boston when the store opened four months ago. I do displays, but I'm really an artist. Actually, I'd like to paint you, but for now your hand will do."

"Which hand?" Here I go again, I thought. Maybe that's what the good doctor meant about my being hopeless.

"Your left. Just relax. Eat. Forget about my being here," she said in an oh so soothing voice.

"American girls are strange. In Germany no young girl. . . . "

"Hildreth, you're forgetting your manners.

This is not Germany. This is New Orleans, and we should be nice to this pretty Yankee artist."

Hildreth resumed cooking my breakfast.

"My name's Sudduth Spencer," I said rising from the stool.

"My name is Malvern Hennessy." She nodded, extended her hand, and moved over one stool.

"Malvern? That's a funny name." I like her, I thought.

"No funnier than some of your southern names." She likes me, I thought.

"This is true," I replied. "Excuse my bad manners. I apologize."

"Accepted." Malvern ordered a coke.

"Have a nectar soda. Hildreth makes the best to be had. You can have a coke anytime."

"What's a nectar soda?"

"Passion juices. You know, nectar from the gods. You'll like it. Trust me." Things were going swimmingly.

"I've never known many northern girls, much less an artist. I've been to England and Europe many times, but never up North. My grandmother believed Bostonians were the only nice Yankees."

"I like your grandmother. We are nice," Malvern says.

"Well, let's say you would have respected her. She could be awesome. She had very high standards. She never let her back touch the back of a chair. That was one standard. She could also be a terror. One time we were on the streetcar going downtown. She was taking me to see *The Prisoner of Zenda* at the Loew's State on Canal Street. Do you know where that is? It's across the street from the Saenger Theatre."

"I've seen the place," she replied. "It looks dreadful, as if it would smell."

"Well, it wasn't dreadful then. It was elegant. All plush velvet and mirrors reflecting crystal chandeliers. Uniformed ushers in hats that strapped under their chins. Just like that boy, Johnny, of 'Call for Phillip Morris' fame. Anyway, it was cold, and she really was something to behold in her long Persian lamb coat, with matching Queen Mary torque and muff. If you ride the streetcar, you know it's possible to sit facing each other if one chooses. Halfway down the Avenue, the streetcar starts to fill up, and this man sits down by me and attempts to start a conversation with her. Now, Nana would help anyone in need, but she didn't sanction talking to strangers. After a while, this man said—and this is the absolute truth, I've never forgotten his name—

" 'My name is Arthur Sawyer.'

" 'Really,' Nana replied. 'Mine isn't.' "

"I loved her though, Malvern. Very much."

"Sudduth, you're wrong. I would have liked her. I like you. I would have invited her to tea and worn a dress and.... "

"You're very nice, Malvern. I like you."

"You're very nice, Sudduth. I like you, too."

I didn't know what else to say, so I started eating. We had been silent for a while when she said, "Look, finished. Didn't I tell you it would be painless?"

"That's very good, Malvern. May I have it?"

117

"No. I really wanted to draw your hand. I wasn't coming on to you. Here, take my card. What I really want to do is paint you. I live in Carrollton. Call me. We'll have dinner and then you can sit while I paint."

She finished her soda, said, "See you, and thanks for the nectar soda. I'm a convert, Hildreth," and walked out. I couldn't help but notice the Elgin movements in her hips. Maybe my libido wasn't dead after all.

"She's for real, Mr. Spencer," Hildreth commented. "Sweet, but in a very business way. You planning on going?"

"I don't know."

"You could do worse. You have done...."

I look sharply up at Hildreth, and she turned and started to clean the grill.

On Wednesday, I called Saks.

"I was wondering if you'd call. Can you come about seven? We'll have dinner, and then I'll begin the preliminary sketches."

"Fine." I took down her address.

Carrollton was named for General William Carrol who encamped there with a force of Tennesseans en route to the Battle of New Orleans. Even today, it still retains much of the reposeful atmosphere of when back, in the 1850's, Carrollton Gardens was a resort of some note, and prominent visitors, like William Mackepeace Thackeray, came to be entertained. George Washington Cable, a native son hailed as a genius even in the north for his heretofore unexplored stories of New Orleans Creole life, used Carrollton Gardens as a setting for the opening chapters of *Kincaid's Battery.*

For whatever reason—and dull detractors would say parties and parades—New Orleans has produced few world-famous authors. And while many have come to observe and write about the city, few have caught its essence, which is the fragility of life.

Anyway, the jewel of Carrollton is its court-house, an imposing structure of brick trimmed with stone, and large white columns which typ-ify the southern courthouse of antebellum days. Today it houses the Benjamin Franklin School. This public school is only for specially talented children and the entrance examinations are said to be awesome. Carrollton Gardens, with its multi-galleried hotel, racetrack, fine gardens (both beer and botanical), was lost when the river shifted its course. Carrollton is the end of the line for the St. Charles Avenue streetcar. It has never been considered part of Uptown.

Malvern lived on a mixed street of long, narrow little houses that are one room wide and seem to stretch back into infinity. We call them shotgun cottages because all the doors open, one behind the other, in a straight line. With all the doors open, one can fire a gun from the front step to the backyard wall without leaving a scratch anywhere. Camphor trees dominated her miniscule fenced yard that was guarded by two Dobermans suffering from chronic diarrhea. The dogs never acclimated to the change from Boston, and Malvern would later be forced to have the dogs put down.

The cottage was clean, starkly simple, and bright with color. It was the first house I had ever been in that was devoid of family and past. And oddly I, who believe that it is excess which defines civilization, liked her taste and her. We had Sangria and arroz con polo. We were comfortable with each other. I can be a perfect gentleman or a perfect rake, and Malvern had not done anything to bring out my rakish side. After dinner we had expresso. Back in her living room, she excused herself and returned with a child's stool.

"Sit here, please," she asked me. "Have you ever posed?"

"No." I said, moving from the comfortable sofa.

"It's important that you not move after I position you, Sudduth. Later we can talk. But, for now you must. . . . "

I didn't have the heart to tell her what a former barber once yelled at me:

"Jesus Christ! Can't you sit still for five seconds?"

I got up from the chair, towel, sheet, and all, and walked out the front door.

"Leroy was having a bad day, Mr. Spencer," the owner said when I returned the things.

"That's no excuse," I told him. "I know all about bad days."

He, who had cut my hair for about six years, never cut my hair again.

Malvern said, "We'll be able to talk on about the third sitting, but for now you'll have to settle for records or the radio."

"The radio will be fine," I said cheerily. "Turn to 1492 AM, it's the 'Way It Was' station. Plays the big band music. Best station in town."

I posed for two hours with two five-minute breaks. I hated posing. No conversation except for "Please don't move." "You're moving." "Please!" "There, that's perfect." "You're moving." "You can't smoke now, Sudduth."

My body began to ache, my legs cramped. I was thinking about my reward, my treat, when the dogs started barking and suddenly this man came through the front door.

"Hi," he said to me. "I'm Russell McClure. You must be Sudduth Spencer. Malvern told me about you. Sorry I wasn't here for dinner, but hotel work is demanding, and I'm still just an assistant manager at the Intercontinental."

So much for escaping into the sins of Egypt. His accent told me he was from Boston too.

"If you'll pull me up, I'll shake your hand, Russell. Posing is hard work."

It really is.

"Tell me about it," he says. "I love Malvern to death, and we'll be married as soon as I get my own hotel, but I can't sit still five minutes."

"Neither can he," Malvern laughed. "You're both hopeless."

We all became friends.

In fact, I attended their wedding and years later when I went up North to Boston for the first time, I went to their house in Newton for dinner with them and their four children. Russell manages the Parker House Hotel, where in

121

1855 the world's first soft roll was introduced that to this day is still known as the Parker House roll.

And Malvern? Malvern paints portraits of sleeping babies and is well on her way to becoming a name. In her small studio hangs, framed, her drawing of my left hand, as well as the sketch from the only time I ever posed, along with many unfinished drawings of Russell.

So, I ended up back at another deb party at the country club. It may be a monotonous life operating with machinelike regularity, but the alternative is too ludicrous to be considered. The big rooms were warm with humanity and the May night unseasonably close. On impulse I went through the long French windows to the flagged terrace, and there I found Kit Kat Carson, now Kitty Wills, alone and crying. Even in the moonlight Kitty was still a stunner. Amazing green eyes and black, black hair, and a mouth generous, crimson, and dimpled at the corners. I walked up to her, put my arm around her, and said:

"The last time we were alone on a terrace was at the yacht club. We were flirting. Remember, Kit Kat? You're even prettier now. Far too pretty to be crying."

"Oh, Suddie, I wish we were back there now. What am I going to do? I'd thought... hoped that Cally and I might.... But tonight, just before I left, he rang. He's going to marry her. She's pregnant. He says he really loves her."

"Maybe she'll give him a cross-eyed and lisping baby," I said, trying to cheer her. "You don't realize how lucky you both were with your children. They're all handsome. You know as well as I that all of Cally's cousins are cross-eyed and lisp."

Kitty laughed the way she once did at the Clubhouse.

"It's true, Suddie. It's terrible, but true. Thank you for making me laugh. It's been a long time. We had such fun, didn't we? Who would have thought I'd ever end up crying at the country club over the fact my husband's going to marry his pregnant whore. Do you ever think about the fun we had and how perfect it all was, Suddie?"

"Yes, but I try not to. It just pulls your heart to pieces and does no good. What's gone is gone. It will never be the same. But think this, Kitty, and it helps. It helps me. We at least had it. Enjoyed it. Treasured it. Remember it. Many don't. They don't have anything. Not even a memory, much less a future."

Kitty kissed me and said, "When did you become so wise? Don't answer that. I know. Will you dance with me and take me home? I came in a taxi."

I took her hand. René had resumed playing.

"One good thing, Suddie, is Cally wants to buy me out of his parents' house. He really loves that terrible old house on Prytania, replete with dadoes, whatnots, and gazebos. I told him it

123

should become a home for indigent cats. He wasn't amused, but he's buying the children and me that jewel of a house on Third Street near the Robinson-Jordan place.

René was playing "Isn't It Romantic."

* * *

9

Baby recaptured my soul the evening of the Knights of Momus parade and ball. She had been gone nearly a year. It was Carnival and night parades add an awesome feeling of mystery to Carnival. The swaying floats are accompanied by black men carrying huge frames of lighted torches called flambeaux, pronounced flam-boo.

Kit Kat Carson and I were at the Pickwick Club for cocktails prior to going on to the ball at City Auditorium. Ever since Kitty's divorce from Callicott Wills, we had been having a splendid indiscretion. We were on our way to becoming.... Well, that doesn't matter anymore.

With ubiquitous plastic cups in hand, we were about to walk through the windows to the private bleachers that put members above the crowds assembled on Canal Street below, when Baby swept into the ballroom on the arm of the obviously smitten Drake Monroe. Drake had become stout since being named a junior partner at Labouisse, Mason, and Mortimer.

"It's Baby!" "Baby's back!" "Drake, you sly dog!" "Kiss me!" "Baby, we missed you!" These were the cries ringing throughout the room.

"Baby looks simply wonderful, doesn't she, Suddie?" Kitty remarked, her arm now locked on mine.

"Look, she's wearing the striped taffeta dress that Victor Costa designed just for her. Remember how he couldn't even talk when they were introduced at the Carpenter party. All she had to do was let her picture be taken for *Town and Country*."

"What?" I absently acknowledged.

"Oh, Suddie, you do so remember. It was after the First Families of Mississippi deb party ... the one held at the Eola Hotel in Natchez the year it reopened. Remember? That girl who heard Calley say she resembled a Mack truck was so hurt that she became one of those awful Episcopal women priests. Remember, you stayed at Percy Sue's sweet house that year. She had a big party the night before the ball and that Texas millionaire's son fell hard for Baby. Didn't she ended up bringing him along to Alma Carpenter's breakfast after the ball? I think it was the first party Alma had at The Elms after she and Leslie divorced and Dunleith was sold. Oh, Suddie, it makes me want to cry that Dunleith has become nothing but a luxury bed-and-breakfast. Why, the Carpenters lived there for generations! Thank goodness Big Alma has managed to hang on to The

Elms. We don't need any more of those outsiders buying our past...."

Would this very sweet woman ever shut up? I thought, but said, "Drake best stop swallowing bread and resume throwing it, the way he used to. Remember?"

"Oh, Suddie, you still love her," she whispered. God, forgive me.

"Looking lovelier than ever" didn't even begin to describe how beautiful Baby looked. Suddenly, it was magic time. It was as if we were all back at the Clubhouse and Baby, once again, the center of the universe for us. You see, to be in love with Baby was to be a member of a club. For a woman to even be in the same room with Baby was to reflect in her glory. That she had defied the world to which she belonged was for the moment forgotten.

"Suddie," Baby drawled. "You look mighty handsome in your new tails. Incomparable fit. You wear tails as well as your daddy."

All I could say before Baby directed her gaze to Kitty was, "Welcome back."

"My sweet Kitty," Baby ran on. "Quick, give Baby a hug. I'm sick about you and Cally. He never did have horse sense for all his sexy good looks. Honey, you're even prettier now than the year you were Queen of Proteus, and after having three children. Why, it's not fair. Is it, Drake? What's your secret? Here, I'm starving...."

"Oh, Baby, hush," Kitty said. "You know you can eat anything. Always could. Gosh, I've missed you. Don't stay away so long. Promise?"

And so it went. A calliope of happy voices.

"Yes," Baby was saying. "I saw them in Spain. They miss New Orleans, of course, but Nada has totally stopped drinking. She's found God. Shingo's so proud. He's loving her like the first time. Where did she find Him? You're terrible, Clayton. You know I don't like irreverence when it comes to God, religion, or me. But, to answer your question, Nada found Him in a nun who found her in a gutter near where she and Shingo are living. Now, she's working at the local orphanage. The children just adore her and she them. Shingo wants them to adopt ten and Nada says it's fine with her. Yes, I really think they will. I stayed with them a month and worked with her. It was very spiritual. Didn't trash out once, but then came London....Well, I never did have the strongest character. I mean, if you're not having a good time, you're missing the point."

This spell of yesterday was shattered when Rayne, she of no morals or heart and of barbaric chic, waltzed in with Bubba Estes in tow. The pain of Baby, Rayne, and Bubba being there was physical: a sensation never felt before. I kept thinking, "Bubba has been divorced three times since the evening he broke my ribs at the country club." It was like a broken record.

The defiant bitch came right up to us and said to me:

"Evening, Spencer. Haven't seen you in a coon's age. Looks like your hairline is receding."

"I hadn't noticed."

"Well, it is," she said antagonistically. "Just think, in a few more years, you'll be as bald as your stuck-up friends."

Intense pain struck me dumb.

"If you had any breeding, Miss Farr, you would know a receding hairline is a sign of good breeding and a trust fund." Baby's voice dripped vengeance. I told you there are no secrets in Uptown.

"From what I've heard, Spencer's trust fund is long gone." Rayne's belligerence would not be silenced.

"That's neither here nor there," Baby replied. "The point is, Mr. Spencer was born with one and, you, from what I have been told, were born 'across the river' with a sign on your chest reading 'Free Admission'. Are you really the ultimate outlet? That's certainly a heady accolade. Just think, if you opened branches, you could cover Dixie like the dew.

"Cat got your tongue, Bubba Estes?" Baby continued. "I'm certainly glad I didn't wear my pearls. Bubba, have you told Miss Farr about the night you broke my pearls out at the country club and Suddie whipped you?" Baby wouldn't stop. "Our former State wrestling champion was about to hit me and missed because of Suddie. That's how Bubba got that knot on his nose. Suddie broke it that night. I think lifting all those weights has affected your brain, Bubba. Pity your brain isn't as large as those still-fine pectorals but, of course, if it were as large, he wouldn't be seen with you, would he, Miss Farr? Am I not right?" Baby had finished.

Bubba grabbed Rayne and propelled the two of them from the room.

I turned to Baby. She was shaking.

"Baby, I...."

"Drake, get me a drink, now," she ordered.

"Baby," I began again. "I...."

"Don't say anything, poor darlin', I owed you."

Baby's unheralded, though joyful, first-evening homecoming was not a harbinger of a return to her former elevated position. Officially, she was welcomed back by people who were polite, civil, correct. By right of birth she would always be included, but the inner *en famille* world of Uptown society comprising the Lower Garden District, Garden District, Uptown, and University was closed to her. From being the first vice-president of a closed corporation, Baby became a minor stockholder.

She had gone too far.

She was also a victim of her own poor timing. Mr. and Mrs. Peabody had died within weeks of each other. Mrs. Peabody's funeral had been two weeks to the day of Baby's return. There were some people who felt her actions had hastened their deaths. (Those wishing to place blame on her behavior conveniently forgot that death is not unnatural when two people are eighty-five and eighty-two.)

Tal certainly didn't blame her. We lunched at Gautreau's on Soniat Street several days after Mr. Peabody's funeral. A devout Catholic, he had entered a seminary to study for the priesthood a few months before.

"You know she was right," he said. "It would never have worked. I know some people feel I should hate her. I never did though. I pray for her. Oh, I was crushed, but I came to realize her way was really the only solution. Otherwise, I would have been in abeyance for Lord knows how long. Perhaps forever. Perhaps like you, Sudduth."

"You know?"

"Yes. I've known a long time," he said.

"I've loved her since I was ten years old," I muttered.

"Do you think she would have socially crucified herself if she had fully realized the consequences?"

"Oh, yes, without any question."

"Why, Sudduth?"

"Because, she believed you to be the 'only truly good person' she'd ever known. She was also afraid of your eyes haunting her the rest of her life and being damned in hell for eternity."

"If only people understood. They don't or won't, though. I've tried. They say I'm too good and change the subject. Are you all right, Suds? You look drawn and down. You know the network even reaches the seminary. Want to talk?"

No one had called me Suds since Country Day. I thought I would cry. Maybe he and Papa were the only truly good people I would ever know.

"No."

"All right. By the way, I'm not selling the

house. I'm leasing it to the church for a dollar a year. Think it will make a fine day care center for children. Couldn't face selling it to outsiders. Perhaps some of Uncle Hambo's brood will want it when they are older."

Baby began to drift and, in doing so, fell from "Vivant" to "Lagniappe." These are the names of the columns that run daily in the society section of the *Times-Picayune*. The difference is rather esoteric. But to meet the present need or requirement, suffice it to say, that "Vivant" covers the remnants of the ancien régime, with feature stories and picture spreads, while "Lagniappe," which means *extra,* is a chatty column chronicling the social aspirations of the new rich.

Baby was being seen with second-string people. People from nowhere. "People," as Narcissa Chambers put it, "whose money's so new they're still making it."

Personally, back to the wall, I would rather be nouveau than never.

She knew the difference. They paid for the honor of knowing her and calling her Baby. She was seen most on the social climbers' circuit. Pay-to-go-to parties such as the Symphony Ball, the Opera Ball, and the other benefit balls of that ilk. If they harbored thoughts of using her for social advancement, they thought wrong. She might play with them, but she never took them to a club, and she belonged to four of the best. Her grandmother had forced her to join Le

Petit Salon, whose membership was aged but ever so soigné. The Orleans Club, whose membership, while not as grand, was a lot more fun and there was no grander place while waiting for a call from Le Petit, should one ever come. The New Orleans Country Club, whose admission fee is one of the nation's highest, she joined (as an adult) with some of the settlement money from the gas company. The Lawn Tennis Club was basically for the young, wild, and free. Her new "friends" had never heard of Colonial Dames or the Junior League to which she also belonged. Junior Leaguers in New Orleans are not afflicted with the locked jaw speech pattern that seems to typify their northern sisterhood.

Baby was still slinky, but imperial had replaced sweet, except when she wished to turn it on. With her own kind, she could still be childlike and winsome. She could also be depressed.

When Baby dropped Hollingsworth Hart, her days of being hotly pursued ended forever, as did the days and nights of jealous fracases.

Hollingsworth and Hart has been our bastion of masculinity since 1857. One might buy shirts at Brooks, but everything else came from H&H. Years of intermarriage had produced Hollingsworth Hart without the ampersand. "Hart" to his friends and "Dear Hart" to his wife, he was a bull of a man. Women were just naturally attracted to his natural hauteur. At fifty-seven, Hart was not unlike Stebo; and like Stebo, he couldn't be trusted to cross the street without succumbing to temptation. He was in his prime when he fell for Baby.

It happened at Alice Foster Lynch's annual hunt breakfast prior to the broadcasting of the Kentucky Derby.

Hart was about to refill his cup from the silver samovar when Baby walked up to the sideboard.

"How do like your coffee, Baby?"

"Alone."

"Not always alone, surely?"

"Unless you're thinking of giving Green Stamps, H&H."

His eyes squinted.

"No one ever called me H&H."

"I'm not everyone, as you very well know."

I put my plate down and walked through French doors to the bar in the hall.

"Remus, fix me a double."

"Yes, Mr. Spencer."

Leila Hart, who had always turned the other way at Hart's quiet peccadilloes, was soon faced with a husband flagrant in his conduct. Hart and Baby were in Bar Harbor, Maine when Leila had the city's top lawyer have him served with papers naming Baby as corespondent.

Baby's memorable reply had been:

"Since when does thirty-seven dinners constitute an affair?"

Leila, in the meantime, had had the locks changed and, on their return, Hart was forced to move to the New Orleans Athletic Club when

Baby wouldn't let him move in with her. When she found out the divorce would leave him with practically nothing, her seemingly callous remark, "I wouldn't look good poor," did not set well. Few knew that Baby needed money herself now.

Yes, Baby's high cotton days were over. Where she had once been a hybrid hovering between two social worlds, she was now about to enter an even stranger third one.

Baby had succeeded in going through Aunt Valkyrie and Uncle Siegfried's money, as well as her grandmother's. Stebo's trust wasn't enough anymore, and Miss Fanny wasn't about to bestow largess. In fact, reports emanating from Highlands were that she planned to leave her money to Oral Roberts.

So Baby became a public school teacher. Baby, who didn't even know anyone who had been to a public school, was going to teach at a very mixed, blue collar, public grammar school. A school in a part of the city to which she had never been: Smoketown. Smoketown Road.

De La Houssaye Etienne Soniat, Baby's second cousin, was the Superintendent of Schools. He "inherited" the position from his father at an early age. As Del (no one ever called him De La Houssaye, except those who presumed) explained to people:

"I had to put Baby where she would do the least damage. After all, I do have some concern for the children of the people of New Orleans. I also have my career to think about. Nepotism

135

can only be carried so far, and Baby isn't bad. She's just high-strung. The children will like her. You'll see."

She threw off having to work by saying:

"I just called United Cab and told the driver to lead the way. After that I knew I could get there. They have a super retirement program and I'll have three months off a year."

The yellow station wagon, flying her Double Queen pennants, looked as out of place there as she.

"These poor little children! God help them!" typified the comments.

Other comments were: "She's lucky. She'd either be raped or lynched in a public high school." Or, "My God, when those children grow up, they'll kill us all."

Another legend was beginning. As the years passed, she would have the highest absentee-ism record in the history of the city's public school system. She was gone so much her second grade class didn't know her or she them. There was the time she arrived hungover in a Cinderella ballgown and told the principal she was setting the mood for her reading of "The Wizard of Oz."

Then there was the time that she left her class unattended to "run to the country club" for four hours. "My body was crying for sun. I mean I was feeling and looking like an albino" and when reprimanded by the principal replied, "Well, I left Zachary in charge. I had to. I was having these truly awful hot flashes and I was just terrified. The change starts early in my family because we're naturally thin-blooded and high-strung."

"Miss Soniat," he yelled. "You teach the second grade, and Zachary is only seven years old."

"Don't you dare use that tone to me. I'll have you know Zachary is very mature for his age, and nothing happened. Did it?"

She may not have known all their names, but they were entranced by her and gave her small presents as tokens of their affection. She in turn would occasionally do extravagant things for them out of guilt. She had no real liking for children, anyone's children. One year she chartered a St. Charles Avenue streetcar to go up and down the Avenue for two hours and hosted the entire class to a party of ice cream, cake, balloons and, some said, punch mixed with champagne. Another time, she took them out to the country club for an all-day spree.

After school, she was either deeply introverted or wildly extroverted, depending on how liquored up she was. Well-calculated bitchery was changing "Little Eva" to "Lady Macbeth" on occasion.

* * *

10

It was going to be a fasten-your-seat-belt night.

"Must we really go to the 1812 Ball?" Baby asked me petulantly.

The ball, given annually by the Society of the War of 1812, celebrates General Andrew Jackson's victory over the English in the Battle of New Orleans, the last major battle of the War of 1812 as well as the most famous. Besides saving New Orleans from conquest by the British, fresh from beating Napoleon, it established the Mississippi as an American river. The siege of New Orleans began in December, 1814 and, on January 8, General Jackson routed the British on the plains of Chalmette. Lancelot Soniat and Horatio Ball were two of the officers who fought gallantly and with distinction. Jean Lafitte, the romanticized pirate, actually did not take part in the battle. His most valuable service was the rendering of seven thousand flints from his private lair. Stebo,

Papa, the Senator— they had all been members of the society that had been founded on the battlefield. I am a member.

"What do you mean 'Must we really go to the 1812 Ball?' It was you who was 'just dying' to go. If I never attended another deb party, it'd be too soon. The girls are getting younger and younger and uglier and uglier."

She snickered, "It's true. They don't have any grace and they're fat for the most part. None of this new crop can compare, even remotely, to me. Even now."

"Baby, we're talking about why you suddenly don't want to go to the 1812 Ball, not your matchless beauty. Those tickets cost me plenty."

"I'll split the cost with you. How about it? No kidding," she said.

"Since when do I take money from you? Anyway it's not the money, which I won't take, it's the principle. You said you wanted to go. Now, you don't. Why?"

"The reason you're poor, Suddie, is because you still think you're rich," she said with an irritating, sidelong glance.

"You bitch! Stop trying to change the subject. Anyway, I pay my bills off every month."

"Oh, I know that. You're very honorable with a Triple A credit rating, but you don't have any savings; whereas I have a considerable amount in my...."

"So I've heard, but that's because you've become notoriously cheap, except when it comes to yourself." She knew I was right and did not reply. "I shouldn't have said that. I apologize."

She wanted to fight. I thought of what Mack used to say: "Chile, you been crying for a whipping all day. Well, now you're gonna get one." Baby was crying for a fight.

"New dress, isn't it?" I asked to change the subject.

"Yes, I bought it on sale. Isn't it stunning? It's a Bill Blass original. I knew it would be reduced because most girls are cows today. If they had any pride, I wouldn't get these wonderful prices. That divine Martha Radelat hasn't forgotten my salad days, she. . . . "

Martha Radelat, besides being "divine," is also lovely, beautiful, and kind. She is the fashion force in New Orleans and head of the couturière department at D. H. Holmes.

Ah, Martha. It was summer. I was in the tail end of my breakdown. God, Cateland and Buck, and Martha finally got me out of it. Alice Lynch was having an en famille dinner party at her Alhambra house out by the country club. Martha walked in wearing a white linen dress bordered with white eyelet. Martha has supreme presence. She was once a model. She tilted her head and smiled at me on being introduced, and said "Hi" in her marvelous throaty voice that is always on the verge of laughter. She has ash blonde hair and skin that makes me think of cream and gardenia petals.

My gloom vanished. My former self returned. My former self always returns with Martha. And soon it was summer's end and we were dancing

141

cheek to cheek at Madewood, the 1848 Greek Revival plantation that had taken eight years to construct and had consumed over sixty thousand slave-made bricks.

Madewood is near Napoleonville on the east bank of the Bayou Lafourche. That's a very long drive, so most everybody had gathered beforehand at the Bayou Bar in the "Ponch" to suitably fortify themselves before boarding the hired buses.

We know how to have fun in New Orleans, know how to make the best of a bad situation. It's said that in England if two people stop to talk, a queue forms. In New Orleans, if two people stop, a parade forms. It's true. The rest of the world has Christmas, New Year, and Easter. We have Carnival, and Carnival runs from January 6, the night of the Twelfth Night Ball, to Shrove Tuesday.

When the time came to board the buses, a riot nearly ensued over who would sit in the back of the bus. For some reason, everybody suddenly wanted to sit on the long seat in the back of the bus. I guess because most of us had never ridden on public buses. The streetcar is one thing. The bus quite another.

"Wish the streetcar went that far," says a voice. "Yeah," screamed another.

Narcissa Chambers yelled, "Why it's real nice back here. Wonderful visibility on both sides, too. I don't understand what all that fussing was about."

Madcap Narcissa's fame as a former Queen of Nereus has been eclipsed by that of her Bloody Marys. She really does concoct the best. I mean

142

there are people who knew Fernand Petiot, the American bartender who invented the drink at Harry's New York Bar in Paris in the 1920's, who still proclaim hers to be the better. Dobbs certainly thought so. He was Narcissa's husband. He's dead now. He drank himself into oblivion. Narcissa mixed his in a red bucket.

I said, "Why don't we take turns sitting on the long seat. It's the only fair way. Everybody should have a turn."

My suggestion passed unanimously. Martha said I was wonderful.

So off we went. Everybody but Baby. Baby arrived via a helicopter belonging to the son of an oil-rich Texan. They landed on the front lawn.

"Leave it to Baby," people said.

"For all her faults, she has style."

"God, what a thoroughbred she is!"

"No," Baby was saying. "We can't stay for dinner, Mrs. Marshall. We have reservations at this fabulous place in Houston. Slim made them over two months ago. It's that famous. Truly. I just wanted to drop in. I'm dazed by what you have done. I just know the place wasn't this grand when it was built by old Colonel Pugh. Becky Prillaman worked with you, didn't she? She has consummate style. So understated, yet madly elegant. Darlin', say good evening to Mrs. Marshall. She's our hostess. Don't know why Slim's so shy. Why, his daddy's rich as Croesus."

"Martha Radelat," Baby said, "This is Slim. Slim Pickens. Actually, his name is Wayne. I can't stand the name Wayne, so I call him Slim.

143

Slim, you remember Sudduth Spencer. Say something, darlin'. Say anything."

I nodded my acknowledgment. Slim was shy to the point of being tongue-tied.

"Martha, that's the most divine Galanos I've ever seen. Why, I just pale being near you. Why, I haven't felt this nervous since I was in the Royal Enclosure at Ascot. You remember? When my most famous picture ran in *Tattler*. Prince Charles came by and asked me if I'd seen Lady Georgina Wellesley. This was before he married. Lady Wellesley is the great-great-great-grand-daughter of the Duke of Wellington. He whipped Napoleon at the Battle of Waterloo.

"I said, 'Sir, if I had, I certainly wouldn't tell you.'

"'Good heavens, why not?' he asked and flashed me this sexy smile. He's soooo good looking.

"'Because if I did you wouldn't be standing here speaking to me,' I replied.

"He grinned and then SHE came up and said 'Charles, I've been searching for you everywhere.'

"'I say! I see what you mean.' Then the Prince of Wales looked at me hard, winked, said 'Smash-ing hat,' and kissed my hand before leaving with HER.

"Sometimes at night, I think what might have happened if she had remained lost. Anyway, I only managed to control myself by touching my Soniat pearls. It took the Soniat pearls to remind me that I was Baby Soniat of Uptown New Orleans and I am a Double Queen. The only one who ever lived too. I felt better after thinking that and having some more champagne. Come on, Slim, it's time to take off."

"Baby's in rare form," I said to Martha. "She puts on a good show."

"I feel sorry for her," Martha said.

I said nothing.

When Madewood's restoration was begun in 1965, the Harold K. Marshalls used a power hose in the Augean manor's main hall and seventy-foot ballroom to remove a twenty-five year accumulation of dirt. That night, though, the New Leviathan Oriental Fox-Trot Orchestra was playing "I Ain't Gonna Give Nobody None O' This Jelly Roll" and in the ensuing stampede to fox-trot, Narcissa fainted. Calm was restored with the more conservative "Mephisto," a ragtime two-step, followed by "Poppy Time in Old Japan." Later, after an enthusiastic rendition of "China, We Owe A Lot To You," there was an impromptu Carnival Ball. Theme: "The Yellow Race."

Two mementoes of that night are in my dressing room. One is a picture of Martha and me dancing cheek-to-cheek and waving to friends. Another is a large watercolor that Martha commissioned as a going away gift for me after Carrebee's was sold.

The watercolor is of me in my dress shirt and black tie, wearing black silk knee socks, patent leather dance pumps, and white boxer shorts.

What happened was this. After we returned to the "Ponch" and I drove Martha home, she realized she had forgotten her keys. Valerie and Mike—Martha's a widow—were spending the night with friends; Martha said the lock on

145

Mike's bedroom window was broken. I said no problem and we headed to the garden. I pulled over two garbage cans, put one inside the other, and turned them upside down. That done, I removed my coat, vest, and trousers and stepped from a garden chair to the top of the cans, feeling like a knight going off to the Crusades; raised the window; hoisted myself up and, as I slid through, the damn window slammed down across my tailbone. The pain was fierce. Then the garbage cans tumbled, hit the chair, and rolled. Well, dogs barked, lights went on, and Martha was about to die from laughter. It was funny. My boxer-shorted rear end was hanging out the window and I yelled for help into Mike's empty room. Somehow I managed to get the window up. To do so, I had to turn over and slide through. I was quite the hero, let me tell you. Everything in life is time and place. Here, again, except for Baby, well. . . .

"Shut up, Baby. Good. That's better. Now, tell me why did you want to go in the first place."

"Oh, I don't know. Maybe I was thinking about Daddy. Remember how handsome he was in his 1812 uniform the year I was presented? Everyone said he looked more like my husband than my daddy. That's why I cut Mama out of the picture. When she saw what I had done, she cried. Those gold epaulets made Daddy's shoulders even wider than they really were, and those tight white leather pants were truly shocking."

I walked to the oversize silver drink tray Baby keeps on a 19th century, neoclassical, mahogany game table and picked up a glass.

"You arrived with chilled Dom Perignon, why are you pouring yourself straight vodka?"

"No special reason. Let's go."

"Oh, all right." She went to get her coat.

"What would you rather be doing?" I asked her black velvet strapless back.

"God knows. I'm bored. Maybe leave New Orleans."

"You'll never leave your setting, Baby. I may have to, but you won't."

She turned. "What are you talking about?" she demanded.

"Oliver's a sick man. He's going to die one day. His family will sell the company. You know that."

"Well, I like that! You'll just up and leave me," she replied indignantly.

"You could come with me. We could marry. Have babies. How about it?" She knew I wasn't teasing.

"I don't want to marry you or anyone. Much less have babies. Anyway, we'd kill each other."

"It's still Stebo. Goddamn him. Won't it ever end?"

I poured another vodka.

"No, it isn't."

"Yes, it is. It's just that it had been a while and I was forgetting the signs."

"Fuck you!"

"Fuck you!"

We drove to the club in black silence. When

147

the attendant opened her door, she jumped out and ran up the red, runner-covered stairs dragging her second best mink coat. (Baby graded everything.)

"What a majestic lion you are," Baby was saying to the over-ninety-year-old General Lucius Quinctius Clay as I entered the ballroom. "Why, it's been years. Not since Grandmère's funeral. I must say though, you just get better looking all the time. No wonder Grandmère told me you were the most notorious rake in New Orleans. She said a young woman wasn't even allowed to be in the same room with you without a male relative being present. Did you really throw a pitcher of ice water on her bosom during a party out at Belle Helene Plantation that time just to see her breasts through the white muslin dress she was wearing? And did you really keep three girls in the Quarter?"

"Delephina was heartless, like you, Baby. Which only confirms my belief that genes talk louder than environment. But, it was lemonade not ice water," he said. "She had been flirting and taunting every man from six to sixty all afternoon. I said, 'Perhaps this will cool you down even if it's lemonade.' She didn't cover herself or run off though. God, no! She stood there, thoroughbred to the core, in front of me and everyone 'til Minnie, her mammy, threw an apron over her and dragged her to the house.

"Delephina possessed the most beautiful breasts of any woman I ever had. They would have honored Helen of Troy. When her engagement was announced to your grandfather, I walked over to his house and shouted for him to come out. He did and I beat the hell out of my best friend. Then I walked to Delephina's and told her. She said I was a fool, that she didn't love me and she didn't love Ravenal, but he had more money than I did. I turned my back on her and never spoke to her again. That same day I joined the army. I always loved her, though, and I had my revenge. She never stopped wanting me. She may not have loved me, but she wanted me. She went to the grave wanting me. Her lust for my body never left her. Not even when she was old. It was in her eyes, that desire for me. That was my consolation. My great consolation."

He turned his white leonine head to me and said, "Sudduth, my boy, good to see you. How's Arabella? Wish she were here. How she and Raiford enjoyed balls and parties. They sparkled. My God, your mother was a beauty. A beauty with a loving and tender heart, though. Tell her I asked about her and send my love. Be careful with this one here. She'll carve her initials on your heart just to while away the time. Here, girl, give an old soldier a goodnight kiss." He bent down and crushed Baby to him to kiss her fully on the lips while his left hand lovingly cupped her breasts.

"Goodnight and thank you, my dear." He bowed and turned away to tell a waiter to get Gilmore to bring his car.

"What a libidinous old man," Baby said, wiping her mouth on her over-the-elbow white kid glove.

"He's no different from Stebo and you were

149

acting like a Quarter whore," I commented matter-of-factly.

"You can go straight to hell," and with that she headed for the nearest waiter with a tray of drinks.

We avoided each other throughout the presentation and did not re-join until the dinner gong sounded and people dispersed hastily, seeking their places as indicated on the seating chart.

Baby's mood had not improved.

"How's the 'no account' Count?" She asked the Count Gillaume de Guillard as we passed him and his recently arrived French fiancée. "You ever get a job?"

Willie, as the Count was called, had chucked his Foreign Office career in a snit over something to do with an island girl and an ambassador's wife. He moved to New Orleans with get-rich-quick schemes. All failed. Now he was going to be married to "a very nice and rich girl of the 'bourgeoise'."

Oh, Baby could be harshly judgmental when it came to others. I thought of the time one of those street people accosted me for money. There we were on St. Peter's Street, having just left that most inner of sanctums, Le Petit Salon. Baby lashed out at the poor fellow. Told him he should be ashamed of himself. Told him he was too young and far too healthy to beg and he should go on a diet. "What woman wants a man with a pot belly?" I gave the man a dollar and pulled her away.

"You know, honey, Mack used to say that

people who live in glass houses should look first at their own backsides."

"I thought they shouldn't throw stones," she replied, trying not to smile.

"Whatever. . . . The point is, don't be such a harsh judge, darlin'. Your own devotion to duty is well known." Her eyes started to get mad.

"We're not going to fight, Baby. You know I'm not being ugly to you. Just where would you be without Del? Answer me that."

"At least I don't beg. Nothing could ever make me beg. Anyway, a quarter would have been quite enough. Let's go play, Suddie. You do want to play?"

Sometimes, though, I do agree with Baby's harsh judgment. Especially when it comes to porters. I mean people are begging, but just try to find a porter in an airport or train station.

Street people really must have a hard time. Just last month, Mother beat one "viciously" with her cane. Mother's seventy-three now.

"Sudduth," she told me over the phone, "All he wanted was a quarter, but I couldn't understand what he was saying because my hearing is so bad now and I was so scared. I explained to him that besides having been mugged twice before, I no longer see or hear very well. I then realized he was bleeding, so I told him to take my handkerchief and twenty dollars. He refused. Said he thought he had problems 'til he met me. Do you think he was being rude?"

"No, Mama, I don't think so."

Well, anyway, Willie and his bride-to-be were not amused by Baby's rather contemptible remark. Nor was I.

"Stop it, Baby. Just stop it," I said. "He may be an arrogant ass, but he doesn't deserve that. Not from you or anyone. You're skating on thin ice as it is. Don't go making a scene when people are finally starting to forget."

"Fuck you," she shot back.

"You must have a death wish. Come on, I'll take you home."

"No, we haven't eaten. Anyway, it's all paid for, isn't it? Christ, we're sharing the table with Judge Hampton and his ugly, tiresome wife. She's cut me dead ever since...."

"Well, try to be sweet to her tonight, Baby. It won't kill you. Just ask her about her health. Nothing is as interesting to her as the state of her health. Be sweet, darlin', and we'll leave as soon as dinner's over. We'll do anything you want. Be sweet. Please. For me," I implored her.

The knot in my stomach was moving. It was alive. Whoever had been charged with table pairing had shown piss-poor discernment. Shit, I thought. Even sane people flee at the sight of the retired Federal Court of Appeals Judge for the Fifth Circuit. Raoul Hampton, he with the suitcases under his eyes, and his wife, Blanche.

A sullen Baby shook off my arm and took a seat. She wouldn't even try, and while I can rise to the occasion even when suicidal, rising to the occasion for two is overwhelming.

Blanche Hampton droned on about how she had been the youngest wife in Uptown to ever go through the "change" which was a lie. I know this for a fact. Mother started the "change" the day before Papa's third funeral. Mama was thirty-eight and the youngest woman in Uptown. Dr. Clifford Uriah Johnson would testify to that, if he were alive.

"Yes, Miss Blanche, I just adore teaching those poor Smoketown children," Baby cooed. "Adore it. It's my life. My reason for leaving my great-grandmother's tester bed every morning. I'm finally fulfilled."

Miss Blanche was frowning.

I kicked Baby and she kicked me back. Why do I fool with her? Do I deserve this? Why do I always forgive? Why do I always forget? I've been forgiving and forgetting all my life.

"Sad about Pontchartrain Amusement Park closing, isn't it, Sudduth?" Judge Ham asked me.

"What, Sir?"

"It was announced on the six o'clock news. The park closes Sunday week. Developers are going to pull it down and...."

Things just keep dwindling away. No one today can appreciate the sheer glory of going to Pontchartrain Park. It was the first place one took a date after getting a driver's license on one's sixteenth birthday. It was where ass-mad youth went on the make; a night fever of lights, assaulting sounds and smells, body heat, and above all, expectation in a Dali landscape; an uncontrolled environment; a raunchy sawdust-atmosphere as totally different from the amuse-

153

ment parks of today as environmentally controlled malls are from a real downtown. There is no sense of place today. That's another thing I have against progress.

I took Baby there the day that coveted green and white card was handed over to me. Daniel had polished the Olds to gleaming perfection, and a ton of chrome was shining as if it were silver. That car had the most sensual upholstery. Some kind of metallic thread that was invisible in the daytime was woven into the fabric and at night it was as if one were sitting in the solar system surrounded by millions of stars.

I remember driving to Richmond Place feeling proud and powerful. Baby and Stebo were out on the louvered-enclosed side porch. The cypress-slanted slats had been pushed open.

Baby's voice could be heard from the sidewalk.

"Faster, Daddy," she squealed. "Faster."

"Evening, Mr. Stebo," I said. "Evening, Baby. Mighty fine night, isn't it?" My voice had changed, but it still broke at an event or happening.

Baby was seated in the middle of this big, white wicker swing. The white voile dress she was wearing was sprigged with tiny red bows and spread over about a hundred crinolines. Stebo, in a white linen suit, was towering behind the swing pushing her. Baby's red spaghetti straps had slipped down over those soon-to-be-celebrated, flirtatious shoulders.

Has anything ever been more erotic than slipped spaghetti shoulder straps? Looking at them gave me a hard-on.

"Evening, Sudduth," Mr. Stebo greeted me rather sternly. "Hear you got a license this morning. Hear you passed written and driving with flying colors."

"Yes, Sir, I did. But how do you know I did well?"

"I called, boy. That is how I know. Do you think I'd let my precious Baby go out with a bad driver? Well, do you?"

"No, Sir. I know you wouldn't."

"Now, Sudduth, I want to make myself perfectly clear. I want Baby home at ten. No later. You understand me? You be very careful with my small queen. Don't go getting her excited. Baby's the kind of beauty that is worshiped, not touched. Understand?"

Stebo's eyes were blue, like Baby's. No one had ever looked at me that hard. I had to make a concerted effort not to blink. He knew that, too, and finally he gave me the renowned Stebo Soniat smile that men called enigmatic, and some women called "orgasmatic" or, if more genteel, "weak-in-the-knees." But, it was Mack who said it all:

"Mr. Stebo Soniat has caused so many hot flashes in good, and bad, ladies, he should buy out Lydia P. Pinkham's and move her to New Orleans."

To me he was always the very personification of a Mississippi riverboat gambler, for all his good blood and breeding.

"You're a fine boy, Sudduth. Now, you children run along. Remember, ten o'clock." Stebo's hands caressed Baby's shoulders and pulled her straps up.

"Tell Arabella I sent my regards. Tell her I said it's time to start living again."

"Mr. Stebo, if I ever need a lawyer, I hope you'll be around to defend me," I said sincerely.

"You honor me, Sudduth. Thank you. I think I'll have a drink." He barked for Carter Grove. (Carter Grove had been named for the famous Virginia plantation.) "Where's your mama, Baby? I haven't seen her since dinner."

"Probably in her room, Daddy."

"That woman stays in her room. I think I'll have two drinks, Carter Grove. Goodnight, children. Remember what I said, Sudduth."

"Daddy really likes you," Baby said as we drove off. "He just worries about me. I'm all he has."

"He has your mama," I interrupted.

"Oh, Mama doesn't count. Why, he'd just die if something happened to me."

"I'd die, too, if something happened to you, Baby," I said. I took my hand from the wheel to squeeze her hand.

"Oh, Suddie, you are sweet. I just love to think about boys dying over me," Baby replied, self-satisfiedly.

That was when the knot that was to grow and tighten in my stomach over the years started forming.

Everybody we knew and didn't know was at Pontchartrain Park that night. Baby was attracting a stream of admirers from the moment we walked through the gate.

We were in the line for the Ferris wheel when I told Baby to stop flirting.

"I am not flirting," she said crossly.

"Yes, you are. Now just stop it."

"I am not flirting. I'm just naturally attractive. Just for that I'm not going to ride the wheel with you."

Baby's voice carries when she becomes excited, and her reply elicited cries of "Ride with me, Baby. Ride with me."

Her cousin, Brumby, was in the line watching. Brumby was already a famous linebacker at LSU. He was a Boulder Dam with muscles, without a mean bone in his body. Brumby was slightly retarded (people said, because his parents had been first cousins). There was a story that during a Tulane/LSU game, Brumby started playing poorly and, at half-time, when Coach Wingfield was berating him, he stopped the diatribe by saying, "I'm sorry, but I dropped my rock." Brumby didn't know his right from his left, you see. After that, a rock was taped inside his right hand. Clemson University stole him from LSU and was so pleased by his performance that he was presented with a convertible. Too ashamed to admit he didn't know how to drive, he ended up wrecking the car and killing himself.

But back to Baby and me at the Ferris wheel.

"Why, I think I'll pick Brumby to ride with me. Will you, Brumby?" she asked, smiling so sweetly at him.

Brumby smiled back and nodded yes.

"If you ride with Brumby, you can go home with Brumby," I said hotly.

157

"You know I can't go home with Brumby. Brum can play ball, but he can't drive," she said triumphantly.

I waited. I've been waiting all my life.

Judge Ham was asking Baby to dance.

"I don't care to dance tonight, thank you," she half smiled.

"Oh, come on. Just one dance, Baby," he insisted.

"No, Judge Ham, I don't care to dance. I don't feel well. Truly," Baby replied.

"Come on. I know you're only teasing. One dance won't kill you," his tone was becoming nasty.

He stood up and grabbed Baby's wrist in an attempt to pull her to him. I rose and put my arm over his.

Baby had been pushed beyond just being cross. She was mad now.

"I said no. Are you deaf as well as boring? If you must know, I don't like dancing with old men. Now, leave me alone. Dance with your wife."

Judge Ham threw Baby's wrist back. People were looking.

"Mrs. Hampton no longer dances." His voice was icy. "Blanche, we're leaving," he snapped at her.

"No need to, Judge, because so are we. Baby?" I said.

"Yes, Suddie, please. I'm very tired. Goodnight, Miss Blanche."

"Well, it was his fault," Baby said in the car.

"I know. I know," I sighed. "But you're digging your own grave with your mouth. Shall I
take you home?"

"Well, I'm damn tired of giving them all a
good show. Let's trash out, Suddie. Let's go to
the Quarter and trash out."

"To the Quarter it is. If you want to trash
out, we really will trash out," I said with finality.

I wondered if we would be alive by morning.

Bourbon Street was the usual Mississippi
of bodies. People resented us. I could read their
minds. "Uptown people out slumming." What
do they know? They know nothing. That river
of lost souls out wandering the streets. Being
on Bourbon Street at night is like looking at the
disintegration of civilization through a twisted
crystal prism.

Raucous laughter...curses...screams...
cries...shouts...jazz, booze booze booze and
more booze. The night ending with no sex, a
malaise of the spirit, and the knowing that God
was no longer in his heaven, at least not for us.

Baby flew to Cozumel the following afternoon.

* * *

11

Just outside Waveland, Mississippi, on the way to Gulfport or Biloxi, there is this huge billboard I must have passed a hundred times, first as a child, driving to paradise on the coast with Papa and Mama ("Are we nearly there, Papa?" "How much longer?" "Son, you must develop patience." "Yes, Sir."), and with Baby or some other proud beauty for a trash-out house party or dance. Spelled out in bold letters is the word SEX. Below this is a message: "Now that I have your attention, what is the condition of your soul?"

The next great attraction after that sign is a rusting, seventy-two foot steel tugboat which was dropped six hundred feet inland by a hurricane. It's been twenty years since Camille and thirty years since Audrey, and the coast is still scarred with abandoned front porch steps that were to lead to paradise and now lead to nowhere. I think of the stoops now as sentinels to pride and to the folly of a "bet-the-cotton-crop" mentality that builds its paradise on sand.

Well, sex had my attention, and the condition of my soul was deplorable.

I had had twenty-two months of deluding myself that I was on the verge of the grand passion of my life when I went to Casamento's for an oyster loaf and beer on that part of Magazine Street that has always been a funky neutral territory where rich and poor can meet in an uniquely New Orleans experience.

Casamento's is the best neighborhood bar and seafood house in the world. Across the street from the Second District Police Station, it symbolizes our "Big Easy." It is opened less than six hours a day, 11:30 to 1:30 and 5:30 to 9:00. It's closed on Mondays and not open at all from June to mid-September. It doesn't advertise. And it doesn't take reservations. Its two small dining rooms, with their gleaming white tile walls highlighted by scrolled and flowered tiles, seat only thirty-three. It doesn't believe in rite privilege. Mayor and store clerk each stand on the sidewalk next to rows of large oyster barrels. Joe Casamento built his restaurant in 1919 and was the boss until the day he died in 1979. His family honors his traditions.

Baby was sitting forlornly at a table by herself. She looked god-awful. The weakest flame I ever saw. Two waitresses were whispering, but we both heard them.

"Girl, what you talking about? I tell you that's not Baby Soniat. And I certainly should know. I remember her from the days when Mr.

Stebo Soniat used to bring her in and sit her on the bar. Pretty as a picture she was, too."

Baby winced.

I had seen her in many spectacles, but never her in spectacles.

"You're going to become a cheap drunk. When did you switch from champagne to beer?" I blandly inquired.

She flared to say something and didn't, but did remove her glasses.

"I was too tired to fool with my contacts. You look wonderful. Come sit with me. I've missed you, Suddie."

"You know my number and it still costs a nickel," I said, looking down at her. My stomach was kicking and my pulse rate increasing.

"I do believe you're beginning to look more like your daddy."

"Tell that to Mama. No, on second thought don't. She always seems to be calling me Raiford as it is. You look awful. Have you ordered?"

"No."

I sat down and motioned to the waitress. "We'll have one large oyster loaf cut in halves, the thick fries, slaw, orange juice, lots of black coffee and lemon ice box pie. And take away the beer."

"Take care of me, Suddie. I'm bad off."

Oh, God. No. Please. I can't. Not again, I thought for a heartbeat. Then I wanted her. Wanted her as always. Would always want her. Wanted to hold her. Wanted to soothe her. Wanted to say, "It's all right now." You see, she was my childless Childe. The only child I would ever love better than myself.

163

Variety is not the only aphrodisiac.

"No one likes me anymore, Suddie."

"Can you blame them, honey? You try people's souls. You take and never give. But I love you anyway. Always have."

"I know. Promise to love me always. I'm worthless, but swear. Swear, Suddie."

"Goose. You've always had my heart, what more do you want? I swear. There now, are you satisfied? Tell you what. After lunch, we'll drive to Covington. I'll ring Dunbar and ask if I can borrow his convertible. Just the two of us. How about it?"

"You never made me a kite. Remember?"

"You have a long memory. Yes, I remember."

"Who took the gold away, Suddie?"

"Life, Baby," I replied. "Life. Life took our innocence."

"Don't call Dunbar. And don't buy a convertible, ever. I hate them. I always catch cold. I'd love to go. It will be like the old days."

"Darlin', nothing will ever be like the old days, but we'll do our best," I said, reaching across to take her small hand.

I made her eat everything and praised God from whom all blessings flow.

And so we began again. Older, but I thought wiser. I was happy. Very happy. My repining had ended with reestablishment of relations with Baby. Baby Soniat was once again the cathexis of my life now that she had double pneumonia. She was really sick. Sick enough for her mother, Miss Fanny, to arrange and pay for Baby to have a private nurse after Dr. Graves called her in Highlands, North Carolina.

Baby had collapsed in Monroe, during the most uncustomary Christmas any two people ever lived through. Baby had initially declined joining me for the holidays at the home of my Johnson cousins because she felt poorly and was not up to the six hour drive to North Louisiana.

Laura and Clifford Johnson adored Baby. Laura had "long forgiven" her for not going Chi Omega. (Laura was active in Chi Omega for over fifty years. Her teas for the Newcomb pledges are still talked about.) The only time Clifford refused to make house calls was when Baby and I visited. Baby called him "Matt Dillon" because he reminded her of James Arness. There was a great similarity. In voice, looks and personality. Clifford called her "Miss Kitty." Baby purred. Around them, butter wouldn't melt in her mouth. Laura always gave Baby the best guest room. Clifford always bought Sweetheart Roses for his mama's favorite cut crystal vase and marched up the stairs with them to Baby's room. Baby was always surprised.

Laura Owen had married Dr. Clifford Uriah Johnson in 1922. Their handsome, red brick columned Forsythe Avenue house faces Forsythe Park, which is a scaled-down version of City Park in New Orleans. This is certainly appropriate, as the most poignant memorial in City Park is the statue/fountain "Unfortunate Boot" that was given by Laura's uncle, Colonel William Frazer Owen, in memory of his young son who died in 1899, aged thirteen, of brain fever brought on from studying too hard. Baby just "adored" the life-like, tousled-haired little boy in overalls holding his "precious boot" afloat to examine the hole, through which pours a stream of water into a pool. Laura had a watercolor of him done for Baby after Baby remarked that the gold medal he had posthumously been awarded certainly didn't make up for never having had a good time. "It's just too sad," sighed Baby.

Baby changed her mind about Christmas, however, when Truza Tremont Schaffer rang from Vicksburg, Mississippi begging her to come to Monroe. So off we went to Monroe. Baby and I would celebrate two Christmases. Christmas Eve, midnight Mass and Christmas with my cousins, and Christmas afternoon with Truza and Elliot. Truza was opening her parents' house in Monroe for one last family Christmas. Come January, she was putting it up for sale. Her father, Tremont T. Tremont, had died two years before. Her mother, Vida Tremont, had been locked up for years, ever since she began going through the change. Mr. Tremont never missed a wedding. Anybody's. He had a *droit du seigneur* complex and loved to fantasize about deflowerment. It was his greatest pleasure and relaxation. It was also said that Mr. Tremont rubbed Preparation H all over his face and body to make his skin tight "just in case" he became lucky.

Truza is Baby's closest friend. They talk at least twice a week when Baby is in New Orleans. They were Kappas at Newcomb. Truza married Elliot Schaffer. He's an obstetrician. They had three sets of twins, four boys and two girls, one-and-one-half years apart. According to Truza, "Elliot's the most fertile man who ever lived. I can't get near him without becoming pregnant. My God, the last time I became pregnant was after his vasectomy."

Elliot never cottoned to Baby and is just about the only man who never succumbed to Baby's fabled charms. Elliot thinks Baby is highly neurotic. Elliot also maintains that Baby "is the most enervating woman God ever created." That's why he opened his practice in Vicksburg.

Well, on Christmas Eve morning, Truza and Elliot drove to the asylum to bring her mother home. Mrs. Tremont had no wish to leave, but the doctors thought it might be good for her, and Truza was insistent that her mother should have a "Christmas Card Christmas" and that her babies should know they had a grandmère. The fact that her mother was crazy in no way deterred Truza. She was intrepidly bodacious.

Christmas afternoon we were seated in the dining room awaiting Mrs. Tremont. We heard their voices in the upstairs hall.

"Mama, please. Carrie Mae and I spent over a month getting the house ready. I want you to see my babies. You have six beautiful grandchildren."

"Kiss my ass, Missy," Mrs. Tremont replied.

Down the stairs they came, Truza pulling her mother all the way. In the dining room Truza beamed.

"Isn't it lovely, Mama, just the way it was when I was a little girl. Are you happy, Mama?

167

Elliot, say something to Mama. Mama, you remember Baby. Baby Soniat. Stebo and Miss
Fanny's daughter. And Sudduth Spencer, one
of my old beaux. Children, this is your grandmère. Aren't they precious, Mama?" Mrs. Tremont
had a strange glint in her wild eyes, one which
reminded me of that mad old tartar, Kahn. In a
heartbeat, she picked up a dinner knife, shoved
it down her throat, gurgled, and with blood
pouring from her mouth, crashed across the
table, face-down in the broccoli aspic.

I mean, talk about a "Christmas Card Christmas." Babies were screaming or laughing hysteri-
cally. Elliot was drinking bourbon straight from
the bottle. Carrie Mae, the cook, was crying out
"Sweet Jesus, do somethin'. Do somethin', Sweet
Jesus." Truza kept saying, "Oh, Mama, how could
you? That was the most perfect broccoli aspic I
ever made, and Carrie Mae and I only this morning finished polishing the silver." Baby placed a
napkin heavy with lace edging over Mrs. Tremont's
blue-haired head. I felt sick, but grabbed Elliot's
bottle of bourbon, told Baby to take the children
to another room, and went to call the police.

"Yes, that's right, Officer. She swallowed a
knife. Yes, a silver dinner knife. No, this is not a
joke or a prank call. Listen, will you please send
an ambulance? No, she doesn't work for a circus.
She's Mrs. Tremont T. Tremont and she's been
locked up for years. Now she's face-down, dead,
in the broccoli aspic."

"Come, children," Baby said. "Let's all go
out on the sun porch. It's such a pretty day. I'll
read to you. One of you go run get me a fairy tale

book. What do you mean your daddy doesn't believe in fairy tale books? Fairy tales are wonderful. They were the only stories I ever read. They're
much better than real-life stories. I treasure to
this day the big book my daddy gave me. I know,
we'll play 'Let's Pretend.' Don't spit on me, Tremont. Why? Because I said so. You did it again.
Tremont. Stop crying. I didn't slap you that hard.
Only sissies cry. Are you a sissy? Well, then stop
crying. Truman, only truly common, little, white-
trash boys stick their fingers in their noses, so
stop. Why, yes, Amanda, I am the only Double
Queen who ever lived. Well, you might be one if
you had a little operation on your eyes. Don't
cry, darlin'. Didn't you know you were slightly
cross-eyed? Being cross-eyed is easy to correct
today. And you do have such lovely hair, just
like your grandmère . . . I know your hair's not
blue. I mean when she was young. It was blonde,
like yours. Yes, a little operation and braces.
Tedo, don't you know it's not polite to stare. It's
considered very rude. You're staring at me because I'm so pretty? Well, you are sweet. You
may sit in my lap for that. No, darlin', you
wouldn't hurt me. No, you can't come live with
me, but you may kiss me. Courtney Ann, honey,
you have truly beautiful eyes, but no one can
see them for those awful bangs. Tell your mama
to take you to a good beauty parlor. That Dutch
Boy cut makes your face appear fat. No, Cade, I
most certainly do not want to see your 'thing.'
Yes, it is nice and certainly big for a boy of your
age, but it's not gentlemanly to show your 'thing'
to girls. Not ever? No, of course, not ever. But there

is a time and place for such things. When? Well, when you marry you can show it. Show it all you want. No, I won't marry you. You're only six years old. Suddie, bring me that bottle of bourbon."

Amanda was screaming, "Daddy, I want an operation and braces so I can be a Double Queen."

Cade was pulling at his daddy's trousers and yelling, "I wanta get married now so I can show my thing."

Tremont was spitting and crying, "That woman beat me for spitting and said I was a sissy. I not a sissy, Daddy."

Tedo kept announcing he was moving to New Orleans to live with "Miss Baby," and Courtney Ann wanted to go to the beauty parlor. NOW.

Elliot was shouting, "Carrie Mae, Truza, somebody get my children away from that Goddamn crazy queen. She's already started to ruin their lives."

"Well," Baby huffed, "I like that," and finished off the bourbon.

Mrs. Tremont was finally carried away in a brown body bag.

"Don't you all use stretchers anymore?" Baby asked the attendants. "They certainly are more dignified. Suddie, I feel so funny. I can't seem...."

The ambulance driver came back and called in for another one to be sent over to the Tremont house on Park Avenue.

"Yes, you heard me right the first time, we need another one, right away, too. No, we don't need a body bag, just a stretcher will do. This one is going to St. Francis Hospital."

170

Baby spent two days at St. Francis before being sent by ambulance to Touro Infirmary in New Orleans.

"Suddie, please get me home. I don't want to die in Monroe."

One evening at Touro, she remarked in a sweet small voice:

"If I die, perhaps I'll become a ghost." She looked seraphically rapturous.

"If you do, please come and haunt me. I'll miss you dreadfully," I said with a deep moan.

This pleased her and she managed a giggle.

"Look what I stole," she said and pulled two surgical masks from under her pillow.

"So you won't get my germs." She put the mask over her mouth, tossed me the other, and mumbled:

"Too sick to play, but please crawl in and hold me. Baby scared."

The born-again-Jehovah-Witness-and-always-frowning nurse was having her supper downstairs.

"You really do love me, don't you, Suddie? That awful and cheap across-the-river girl, you never loved her? Did you?"

"Yes, I really love you. Even if you are hard to love most of the time. Don't know how you can doubt it. As for the other, don't debase the word love. I didn't even really like her."

Baby's phoenix-like recuperative powers had waned. The Baby I carried from Touro Infirmary was melting away.

"I very nearly died," she said matter-of-factly once settled in the car.

When I did not reply, she closed her eyes.

Curled in Solidel Soniat's great tester bed, Baby most resembled a lost kitten. As I adjusted the eiderdown, she looked at me and asked:

"You love me even when I'm my most bad. Why?"

Before I could answer, she was asleep.

Baby refused to talk to or see anyone but me. I saw Baby every day, and sometimes twice a day, during her recovery. It was the longest period of uninterrupted happiness I ever experienced with her. The knot in my stomach stopped moving and I stopped drinking. I usually arrived as the nurse was leaving and stayed until eleven. For weeks I had heard her say "That child's just about worn out."

Baby's once disapproving nurse now couldn't do enough for her. Mind you, this was the same nurse I had taken to a fine dinner á deux, at Baby's insistence, and whose only comment had been: "Thank you. The water was delicious." Her very controlled "Goodnights" had progressed to "You take care, Miss Soniat," which in turn had progressed to "Take life, honey." This is a favorite expression of Linda Noe Laine's, Governor Noe's baby daughter. It is her philosophy. Baby had confiscated it when Linda moved to San Francisco.

Most of the time Baby would sleep, lost in the great bed, watched over by me. I would be at peace, finding contentment just by being in her presence. Besides Baby, the only thing in the bedroom I really liked was the Aubusson, with its faded roses. The carpet had lain on the floors of Belle Helene plantation, where peacocks once strutted and cried out, and which is lost beneath the implacable river.

Even I, who believe that it is the excess that defines civilization, found the surroundings claustrophobic with their "fitting tributes" to a beauty that is worshiped. Her dressing table, heavy with muslin, lace, and grosgrain bows, displayed silver-backed brushes, combs, and mirrors as well as silver boxes and flagons of scent, picture frames and other accessories wrought by skilled silversmiths. Her Venetian silver looking glass most resembled the one to be seen in that most English of houses, Knole, the Sackville-West house in Kent. Muslin-draped windows were swagged with lace and more grosgrain bows. But it was her bed cover that was vanity glorified. Pink velvet, specially ordered to match the color of her lips. Baby was truly vainglorious about her lips.

"Daddy told me before I could walk that I would never have any need for lip color. He said my lips were the most vibrant and perfect pink he'd ever beheld and since finding out about the many lips Daddy beheld, I know he didn't exaggerate."

Crowded, cluttered, and overdone, it was woven from a web in childhood. As Antoine de Saint-Exupéry knew:

> *It is only with the heart*
> *that one can see rightly;*
> *What is essential*
> *is invisible to the eye.*

On other nights, the bad ones, I would read

to her from a large tattered book of fairy tales inscribed "To my small queen, from Stebo."

In retrospect, why not? Weren't we all reared to expect happy endings? And don't we still expect happy endings even if we only survive by trying to keep our lives from becoming too tawdry? Perhaps we were the last generation reared on "and they lived happily ever after." Am I not searching for the happy ending as a seeker of the unattainable in love?

Yes, I was happy during Baby's convalescence. Very happy. She said "I love you" for the first time, and perhaps she really did. However, "in love" is the reverse of knowledge. In fact, one could say, it is refutation of knowledge. And every night I refuted what I knew and what was written in Baby's treasured book.

Our engraved invitations from Pierrot Villere were the first thing to pique Baby's interest.

"We can go, can't we, Suddie?" Baby asked in a pleading small voice. She was really excited for the first time in months.

"We'll go if Dr. Graves thinks you're strong enough. Deal?" I said, smiling down at her.

"Deal, it is, darlin'," she replied.

That evening, she began looking for the keys to a trunk stored in the luggage room and asked if I would bring her the bolt of hand embroidered silk brocade that her Aunt Valkyrie had bought in China years ago.

"What are you planning, Baby?" I asked. There was a slight movement in my stomach.

"All my gowns are strapless. A good chill would kill me for sure this time," Baby explained. "Also, I don't want people to see how thin I am. I honestly don't think my breasts could support a dress. If the silk hasn't rotted, I'll have Mr. Seoane come by and fit me for a Chinese mandarin with a high collar, long sleeves, and deep slits. My legs are still good. I'll show them instead."

Uptown's most esteemed tailor, Manuel Seoane, was duly called and arrived with his assistant, Amelia Broussard. Mr. Seoane is from Alicante, Spain. Tailor International on Prytania Street has been favored by Uptowners since almost the day his double doors opened. Mr. Seoane is a wizard. He's so good that suits I buy in Washington I have posted to him for alterations. He and Amelia are friends. Just three months ago, when Amelia arrived in Washington for her niece's wedding, I was invited, attended, and had a super time. Anyway, Mr. Seoane says New Orleans and Spain are the same in that true aristocracy is what's left over from rich ancestors after all the money is gone.

Well, Mr. Seoane deemed the silk virtually irreplaceable, fashioned a dress that masked Baby's thinness and temporary loss of bosom, and a reluctant doctor said yes, with reservations, stressing no drinking and an early evening. Baby was as excited as a child. Her shell-like ears turned pink for the first time in years.

The much anticipated night finally arrived for Baby, but the incessant rain of now over a week would not abate even for the House of Villere. White-coated parking attendants tunneled the sidewalk with golf umbrellas in the colors of Carnival: yellow, green, purple. The house blazed with lighted candles justifying its aura popularis as "the house of a thousand candles." Walking under the enclosed canopy that ran from the street to the worn marble entrance steps, who could have conceived that this would be the swan song for the big house?

The reason, however outlandish, is true. It seems that between parties and proposals, Pierrot traveled. Now, when Pierrot traveled, she played bridge. When she played bridge, she played for high stakes. The higher the stakes, the higher her orgasm. That's how she got off. Pierrot was basically frigid. I told you there were no secrets in Uptown. Well, obviously she didn't get off that much because, when she expired from a massive embolism, she was screaming TRUMP, and Brandt's mountain of money was a molehill.

"Thank God I had the sense to remember Aunt Valkyrie's silk and have this dress made. All this dampness has actually chilled me to the bone," Baby was saying as we passed through the immense doors that would have accommodated an elephant carrying a gadi-seated maharajah.

Pierrot's parties were always the talk of Uptown. Baby and I were weaned on them. That night there would be jazz bands in the tented garden and jazz bands on the enclosed front and side galleries. The wedding cake house, built in 1889 at a cost of $250,000, would blaze like the Titanic on its maiden voyage.

The Villeres, in their own right and through "royal" marriages, have produced more Consorts to Rex than any Uptown family. It was a legacy that made outsiders obsequious.

The "one and only" Pierrot had been a queen as well as *Town & Country*'s June cover bride of 1944. Brandt Villere had been crazed for his petitely beautiful wife until, it was said, a tattered copy reached him in Italy. He read the interview and realized his pride had no heart, much less common sense.

"It will be so wonderful when this tedious war ends," she had been quoted. "Our garden's going to ruin and there are no boys to dance with at the country club."

According to his lifelong friend, Perry Wickham, who somehow ended up in the same foxhole, Brandt was so hurt that he cried for the first time in his life. There he was, fighting to save the world for his young wife and unborn child and she didn't even miss him. Whether he saw the land mine, no one will ever know, but the next day he was blown to Kingdom Come.

Two months later, Little Pierrot weighed in at eleven-and-a-half pounds. Poor Little Pierrot, all her life she was to hear her mother's scratched mahogany voice saying: "Look at her, will you. That fat child nearly killed me."

Perhaps if Little Pierrot had been a child to be proud of, her mother's attitude would have been different. While she did have her mother's delicate features, her face was square, like Brandt's, rather than oval. Instead of a blonde mane to be celebrated, she had inherited her father's tangled mass of coarse black curls and, most unfortunately, his thick stocky-framed body. Pierrot knew instinctively that the child's personality would never attract a moth and that she would never learn the art of living.

As the last of the Villeres, Brandt left his family mountainously rich with old money. Pierrot became the richest woman in New Orleans and the city's most beautiful Merry Widow. Black was so becoming that she was never to return to pastel colors. She would deviate only in the summer and then only to black and white.

The "tedious war" finally ended and Pierrot soon forgot she had ever been married and, more regrettably, that she had had a child. Little Pierrot had been handed over to Delores immediately after her arrival. In fact, it was Delores' niece, Ruby, who suckled the infant in the nursery rooms that sprawled over the top third floor.

Poor Little Pierrot. We never thought about her except to feel sorry. Her mother had her head shaved in hopes it would grow back straight, which it did, but it took forever. Throughout our first two years at Country Day, Little Pierrot was bald underneath her hand-crocheted caps and withdrawn. She was also fat. Delores, who really loved her, fed her candy to compensate for her lack of hair.

Poor Little Pierrot. There are many queens in New Orleans: Quarter queens and Uptown queens. Little Pierrot Villere was the only Uptown queen who never longed for, or even desired the crown, much less the mantle. It was just preordained.

"That child will be a Queen of Carnival, even if it kills her," Pierrot widely proclaimed.

Poor Little Pierrot. Her dress was ordered one year before the announcement and she was withdrawn from school to undergo a transformation and locked in the nursery to prevent her stealing food. The nursery had been converted to a gymnasium and a retired female Marine sergeant hired to supervise her workouts. It was rumored that Little Pierrot's lower ribs were removed to give her a waist, and her upper and lower back teeth extracted in an attempt to give her cheekbones. Her gown was not being made to fit her. She was being remade to fit her gown. And fit it, she did.

The federacy of Villere money and Pierrot resoluteness metamorphosed Little Pierrot into a swan worthy enough to be Queen of Carnival. Inside herself, however, she was the same withdrawn child from Country Day and long-ago birthday parties in her nursery where she would hide from us and not be missed until it was time for us to leave. Poor Little Pierrot. She was still white bread and skimmed milk, and no tomcat wants skimmed milk when he's surrounded with so much cream just dying to be lapped up. No tomcat, that is, but Joper Stokes, and Joper could have been hired to bore the English Channel.

Baby was in her element. How she gloried in attention and being once again fussed over. The sapphire solitaire in my pocket burned. She was cresting when she was eclipsed by the storm turning violent. It may not have been the hurricane season, which is autumnal, but whatever the storm was, it was an excellent imitation of a bad one. The wind rose to a gale, hurling itself up the Avenue, thrashing at everything in its path. The old house was moaning when the silver-gray hood of Bubba Estes' classic 1936 Rolls-Royce sliced through the garden tent like a razor blade. As the tent collapsed, a gusher of collected rain drenched candle-lighted tables where, just moments before, guests had been seated or dancing. The first-floor rooms now boiled with people no longer laughing. I decided to take Baby to the nursery. We had reached the landing window seat when a ripping shriek made us turn. The entire enclosed canopy had been wrenched from its moorings and blown to the top of the Andrew Jackson Apartments where it remained "draped" for a week.

"I hate storms. They always scare me," Baby grumbled. "You know that, Suddie. This has been the most awful party, and I'm sure it cost more than the one that was given when Little Pierrot was Queen of Carnival. God, the whole thing has been positively manqué."

"Darlin', I have no control over storms that become hurricanes," I said in an attempt to soothe her. She's such a child. She misses being the center of attention.

"Baby, we shouldn't be standing by this window. Come on, let's go on to the nursery. Maybe we can find the rocking horses. You used to love to ride the largest one, sidesaddle."

"I thought the nursery was converted to a gymnasium to make Little Pierrot pretty," Baby sighed.

"I know, honey, but perhaps some traces of what's left of our childhood remain. If Delores were alive, she would have plates heaped with good things for us. 'Member? Come on."

"Oh, all right, Suddie."

My proud patrician beauty was tired. Why do I always make excuses for her? I touched the sapphire solitaire in my pocket for luck.

The stairs to the third floor were steep. We didn't hear their voices until just before we reached the nursery door.

"But Mama," Little Pierrot cried, "Joper's ugly. He doesn't even have two eyebrows. He must be the only person in the world with one long, hairy eyebrow running across his forehead."

"Have you not ever heard of electrolysis?" Pierrot was screaming at her. "Don't you know when a man's passion is up, a woman can get him to do anything? You could have plucked the area above Joper's nose. Yes, plucked! Plucked with a pair of tweezers from Walgreen's. He would have loved it. Believe me."

"Mama, it's not just the eyebrows. Joper talks funny. Like he's trying to be an Englishman. Why, everybody knows he's from Lafayette."

"There's nothing wrong with being from Lafayette." Pierrot's voice was deadly controlled. "His family is Confederate Episcopal and if their money's not that old, it's old enough. Certainly old enough for the likes of you.

"I've spent a small fortune on getting you settled, and you turn down Joper. Your ugly old shape is returning and nobody else has shown the slightest interest in you. Not even that once-

181

overdeveloped Bubba Estes. This was to be your engagement party. Did you even look at the ring Joper had for you? Now he's gone. Gone for good. What a disappointment you are. I wish you had never been born. You really do disgust me. Get out and leave me alone. You deserve to be poor. You'll be sorry. Just you wait. Did you understand me, Pierrot? I said get out."

"Mama must be crazy," Little Pierrot said to us in short, audible gasps of breath as the door closed with force behind her. "She says I'll be poor if I don't marry Joper. What's Mama talking about? Why, we're rich. Everybody knows we're rich. We've always been rich. I can't stand Joper Stokes. I'd rather be dead than married to him."

And die she would. Poor Little Pierrot. After Pierrot's death at a bridge table the next summer, the Villere palace was sold. There was just enough money for Little Pierrot to buy a dreadful, banal house on the lake side of the Avenue and keep her mother's red MG running. One day she drove to the Sunshine Bridge about seventy-five miles west of New Orleans. The bridge is Louisiana's greatest folly. A brilliant white network of huge steel beams that crosses the Mississippi at Donaldsonville, and most resembles a child's erector set, it is a thirty-one million dollar bridge from nowhere to nowhere.

Jimmy Davis, our twice former governor and songwriter/actor, built the bridge during his second term and named it Sunshine after his most famous song: "You Are My Sunshine, My Only Sunshine." Governor Davis spent more time in Hollywood than in Baton Rouge. But times were simpler then. A governor's main job was to entertain, amuse, govern, and not get caught.

A neighbor said that when little Pierrot drove off in the fading red MG with the top down, she was singing to the top of her lungs for the first time, ever.

"I'm so happy today," she had told the woman, "that I don't even mind not having the money to have the radio repaired. Why, I'll just sing to keep myself company." She pulled off singing, "You are my Sunshine, my only Sunshine, you make me happy when skies are gray. You'll never know dear how much I love you, please don't take my Sunshine away."

Her car was found parked in the middle of the bridge. There never is any traffic. Her body was found a week later.

"Oh, God. Suddie! Everything is terrible. Please get me away from here." Baby moaned. "Heaven knows when those attendants will return. I'd walk home, but I'm too weak. We're not that far from my place. You could walk there and drive back in my car. I didn't lock the door and you know where I keep my keys. Would you? Please. For Baby."

"Have I ever denied you anything? I'll go if you'll rest in one of the second floor bedrooms. Deal?"

"Deal, my sweet Suddie."

We walked back down the steep stairs to the Mallard Room, and in a Mallard bed, Baby went immediately to sleep. Prudent Mallard, a native of Sevres, France, had carved from Central-American rosewood or palissandre furniture which would become among the most rare and expensive of antiques. The Mallard Room housed his most elaborate and famous dressing table, the "Duchesse," a great four-poster bed, and his finest armoire, as well as mahogany chairs and settees.

Outside, the rain had checked itself, not that it would have mattered. I made my way down the Avenue, struggling against a half-gale which bent the trees and took my breath. Grit stung my eyes. The wind was a tangible thing, pressing against me—legs, thighs, back, chest—like a wrestler striving to throw me. Like that time at the country club.

I could have kissed the yellow Ford station wagon when I finally entered Baby's garage. Driving up the Avenue to Pierrot's, I kept beeping the horn to hear "Mary Had A Little Lamb."

Back at Pierrot's, I pushed through the crush of people, now more than ever ready to trash out, and ran up the wide stairs to Baby. My vulnerable child was in a deep sleep. Cradling her in my arms, her head next to my heart, I made for the stairs. I had just left the landing and was starting the final descent when a drunken Bubba Estes staggered from the library. Bubba had had a breakdown after Brian Berke usurped his legend. His chest had finally fallen, and he was on his way to becoming grossly overweight. From my position on the stairs, I could see a bald spot through his combed-over hair. His fifth wife is the worst or the best of the lot. Who knows? Who cares? Looking up, Bubba stopped and turned to his wife:

"Joe Lyne, look there. I want you to see the famous Baby Soniat."

"The 'famous' Baby Soniat?" Joe Lyne asked somewhat awed, as if Baby were a myth and not merely mortal.

"Yes, that's the one. The arrogant bitch has passed out. From what I hear she's on her way to becoming a lush. Just like her arrogant daddy. So high and mighty they were. She was too good to even dance with me, once."

And so it came to pass that on the cele-brated Villere staircase I beat Bubba Estes twenty something years after the fact. Beat him without laying a hand on him. Beat him with a look. A look I had appropriated from the Senator. A look used by him only when he was most displeased. A look that I had only used once, years before, on a professor at Tulane with whom I had been having a running battle concerning my cavalier attitude toward his lectures.

The morning he reassigned me to an empty back row seat far removed from friends and proud beauties was the day it happened. The day before Belle Bancroft and I had been ordered from his classroom for flirting. After the bell, as I ap-proached the door to leave, I turned and gave him the Senator's look. Its effect was like a bolt of lightning. Rushing at me, he grabbed and threw me against the wall and in a voice so tightly con-trolled and thin I thought it would break, said:

"Mr. Spencer, If you ever, and I mean ever, look at me that way again, I'll kill you. Do you

185

understand me, Sir? I'll kill you. I swear to God."

I mean, this Yankee geology professor was pissed. I felt good. Real good. He was shaking and the veins in his neck were throbbing.

"I shan't have to, shall I? We understand each other now," was all I had said.

He broke his fist on the wall and returned north at the end of the year. I think I made either a B or the "Gentleman's C" in geology. Years later, my old tennis partner, Dagg Hillyer, encountered him in New York. He was teaching at City College. His first question to Dagg was:

"Tell me, is Sudduth Spencer still alive?"

Well, the effect of the Senator's look on Bubba caused all color to drain from his face and, dropping his glass, he hastily retreated back to the library, leaving Joe Lyne looking very sad and giggling nervously.

"My sweet, dear, Suddie, thank you," Baby whispered on reaching her damp apartment.

"Light a fire, darlin', while I change. I'm so cold. Why, I'm freezing to the bone. I don't think Dr. Graves would object to my having some brandy. Do you?"

"I don't think so. You go change. I'll try to start a fire. The wood's wet. You never remember to close the damper."

A pale Baby came from the bedroom lost in a tan cashmere robe that enveloped her, collapsed by the sulky fire, and reached for the snifter in my hand.

"Whatever possessed you to buy a robe about twenty sizes too big?" I said, smiling down to her upturned face.

"It was Daddy's. I wear it when I'm most cold. I stole it from the pile of his clothes Mama gave Carter Grove. It still smells of him. I've never had it dry...."

"Baby, I ... we have been so happy these last months. You know how I feel about you. You've always known. Marry me. Please. I love you so very much. You know, I'm basically monogamous."

I put Nana's large sapphire solitaire engagement ring in her lap. Baby just sat there looking down at the ring.

"Well?" I said.

"It's beautiful, Suddie. Truly. Why, I can still recall how lovely it was on Miss Eva Elizabeth. She had the most graceful hands and was so regal. I'll never forget the afternoon she had that tea for me and how the strawberries were reflected in the silver. That was the year I came out. She told me that true manners is how one eats when one is alone. Why, she was royal, like Queen Ma...."

"Baby, we're not discussing my much-lamented and sainted grandmother, we're...."

"Darlin, I told you I loved you. Isn't that enough?" she said listlessly.

"No, it isn't, Baby. Not anymore. Don't you see we're too old now just to be playmates. I'll not have you go jerking your chin, Baby. I'm not talking about that kind of old, and you know it. To me, even at ninety, you'll always be the most beautiful girl to ever have led a cotillion. But, even beyond love, we are the same, Baby. The same blood. The same memories. Memories no one else has. If you would just let go and marry me. No one will ever love you better. No one could, and know you."

"Well, I'm sorry, Suddie."

"So am I, Baby."

"I never told the others I loved them," she answered somewhat sullenly.

"Fuck the others! What am I supposed to do? Go on pumping for my life twenty-four hours a day over you?"

"Is it so bad?"

"No, it's not bad. It just kills me. Can you understand that? It kills me. It is killing me."

Her voice was like a disembodied spirit.

"I think I'll go to New York. I can stay with that darlin' girl on Sutton Place. You know, the one you think resembles Margaret Truman. I would go to Washington and stay in Georgetown with Debra and Jack London. They're fun and I love them, but right now I would pale beside her. She's a beauty too, and I certainly don't need paling in my life now, or ever for that matter. Remember the time you jumped out of somebody's automobile to stop that airport bus for me? Why you practically had to throw yourself in front of it to get the driver to stop. I can still smell the burning rubber of the tires as he braked. Where were we, Suddie? I forget."

Baby can be dressed and ready to move off on a jaunt quicker than any man or woman alive. She is the perfect person for expeditions and fun mainly because she has magical hair. All she ever needs to do is toss or shake her head and it's perfect. Even after wearing a hat, say for four or five hours on a hot, humid day. Expeditions and fun. Nothing else, I thought.

"Goodbye, Baby," I said as I reached down to take the ring from her lap.

"Night, darlin'."

* * *

12

I was thinking about expeditions and fun as I descended into a dungeon so deep I had no wish to escape. Sadness interspersed with tinges of happiness sank toward a nadir of misery. Baby's Marie Antoinette complex had finished me. That's how I ended up in the St. Thomas Housing Project at three in the morning, resplendent in white tie and tails, a silk top hat, a velvet-collared herringbone coat, white kid gloves, and the Senator's white silk, fringed evening scarf.

Leeds Weber's death was my justification for going there. Leeds had actually been dead for years; it was just that nobody had bothered to tell him. The bloated, ghost-white old man, who drank away his life in rather dreadful rented-by-the-month motel rooms in preference to his family's high-ceilinged iron lacework house on Chestnut Street, left all his money to the Louisiana State University wrestling team. Now that was cocktail conversation for months, let me tell you! He was forty years old.

Airplanes had been the only things to make Leeds happy. Airplanes were his passion. He would charter planes for himself, fly to wherever, check into the best hotel, and stay drunk in his suite for a week. It made him happy for a little while and made his family frantic. They were always trying to have him committed.

Baby was waiting for me to unlock the car door when we heard Leeds' licorice drawl.

"Where y'all going?" His driver brought the Lincoln Town Car to an abrupt halt and Leeds leaned out the window. He was only semi-drunk.

"We're going to Ruth and Longer's, Leeds. They're having an engagement party for Boopie and Henr...." He cut me off.

"Howdy, Baby. You sure do look nice. Real nice. What's that thing you're wearing?"

"This 'thing,' I'll have you to know, is a quilted skirt," Baby chided. "The woman you see with the flowing hair is Salome doing her dance of the seven veils for John the Baptist. It's an exact copy of an Aubrey Beardsley illustration. Beardsley was a famous English designer. I think his sensuous, rhythmic style and dramatic drawings suit me nicely. Don't you, Leeds?"

Leeds knew she was making fun of him.

"I just bought me a airplane," Leeds replied.

"Did it come with a pilot? You'd really be a menace in the air." Baby laughed at him. "Why, I couldn't sleep at night for worrying."

"Ain't you something," Leeds chuckled. He talked country because he hated pomp and circumstance. He was only comfortable with trash. He had already broken his father's heart and now he was working on breaking his mama's. All the Webers are strange in one way or the other. They suffer from the "bet-the-cotton-crop" mentality. Leeds' third cousin took an axe to his mother and stepfather. Only his stepfather survived. The boy couldn't wait to inherit. He's in jail for good. At least everyone hopes so. His grandmother, Camilla de Chalfont, who is refined quite beyond the point of civilization, has been in seclusion ever since, with what is now said to be over two hundred cats. At least that's what Mama's vet says and he should know as he is always making house calls. The Chalfont house on Coliseum Street near Audubon Park is so heavy in wisteria-draped lavender and Dorothy Perkins roses that the whole place sags and people think it's going to collapse.

"Come out to the field with me and have a look. Come on. Jump in. I'll have Sidney bring us back. Baby, tell Suddie you want to see my plane. Hell, what's another party to you two? Be late. They probably have four hundred people coming."

"Do you want to go, Baby?" I asked.

"Not really, Suddie. But it might be fun. All that money is certainly wasted on him. Oh, let's go. Why not?"

"We'll meet you at Shushan Airport, Leeds. OK?"

"No, it isn't, Suddie. I want to enjoy you two

now. Come on! Hell, this piece of junk I ride around in has an ice box packed with champagne and fancy Russian fish eggs. Y'all be back in an hour. I promise."

We got in. By the time we reached the field the champagne and caviar had made us more convivial than we really were.

We were having drinks in the plane's fancy cabin when I heard the motors turn.

"Leeds, what's going on?" I asked rather sharply.

"Nothing, Suddie," he said with a Cheshire cat smile. "My pilot's just checking the engines. Didn't I tell you I'm going to Norfolk, Virginia for dinner with a former school friend and then on to Mexico? You could go with me. Why not?"

Baby looked at me.

"Let's go, Baby," I said.

"You used to be a sport, Suddie," Leeds derided.

"He still is, Leeds," Baby fired back. "You've just become a tiresome drunk."

"Baby, be quiet. Come on."

It was too late.

Leeds pulled a gun out and said "Better fasten your seat belts. We're about to take off."

The flight to Norfolk was long. The gun just seemed to put the final damper on things. When we finally landed, Leeds called his friend, who regretted he was unable to dine. It seemed he and his wife were leaving for the hospital. She was about to have a baby. In fact, her water had burst.

"Looks like I'm stuck with you two for dinner," Leeds sneered. "Hell fire! That will be no fun. I'll just go on to Mexico."

"Leeds, we have no intention of going to Mexico with you, understand," I said.

"Who said anything about you two stick-in-the-muds going to Mexico? Hell, I'm not even taking you back to New Orleans."

"What!" Baby and I said in unison.

"That's right. I like people who amuse me. You two ain't fun anymore. Bye, y'all. Start walking."

He marched us down the steps, shut the door, and flew off, leaving us in the middle of this runway that is in a field, miles from anywhere, judging by the blackness of the surrounding countryside.

"Suddie, what in the world are you going to do?" Baby is not a feminist. "Maybe we should have gone to Mexico."

"As I recall, darlin', we weren't invited," I reminded her. "Let's go to that prefab office I saw when we landed."

"I'm cold, Suddie."

"I know, darlin'. Come on," I said as I helped her put on my jacket.

"Do you think anyone is in there, Suddie?" Baby asked.

"No, because I don't see a car anywhere. But there might be a phone if we can get in. At least you'd be warmer."

The door was not locked and there was a pay phone on the wall. The interior resembled a hospital waiting room. Everything was hospital green. A way station for death.

195

"Baby, I don't have any change. Give me a nickel, honey."

"I don't have any nickels. You know I hate change. I always put any in my carousel bank. The one Daddy had carved for me on my seventh birthday by this German man in the Quarter. Daddy took me once to meet him. He said I was the most beautiful little girl he'd ever seen. A perfect Aryan. I do so love my bank. Especially when it revolves and plays 'If Ever I Cease To Love' when money's dropped inside. Daddy would drop coins in it every night 'til I went to sleep. Once a year I take it to the Whitney and this sweet man counts it out and gives me dollars. I look forward all year to going. Anyway, it costs a quarter here. See that sign. Can you believe it? A quarter. That really is outrageous."

"Baby, do you have any money at all?" (I already knew the answer.)

"No. Why? I never carry money when I go out with you or any man, for that matter. Oh God, Suddie! How much money do you have?"

"Fifteen dollars," I replied.

"Do you know anybody in Norfolk, Suddie?"

"No. Do you, Baby?"

"No. But, I once met Mrs. Douglas MacArthur at a party held at the Waldorf-Astoria. She lives there. In an apartment. I think her husband, General MacArthur, was from Nor. . . . "

"Darlin', not now." I wonder if any more planes will land? I said, speaking to myself.

No more planes landed. I removed plastic cushions from the two chrome armchairs and made a pallet for Baby. I slept on the floor by her. It was a long, cold night.

Around five, Baby woke me up with her screaming. I jumped up. This man was standing over us holding a foul-smelling mop.

"Who in the hell are you?" I asked him.

"I'm the janitor. You and she sure are sound sleepers. I been here for twenty minutes. What you doing here? Where's your plane?"

"You won't believe this," I began. When I was finished, he just shook his head.

"Tell you what I'll do. I'll drive you two to the airport when I'm finished. It should be open by the time we get there."

Sure enough, the airport was just opening. In fact, Delta, which was founded in Monroe, Louisiana was the first counter to open.

"Suddie, we don't have any money," Baby said. "They won't let...."

"Trust me, Baby. Have I ever failed you? I'll get us back home."

We walked to the counter and I introduced myself to this oh so pretty and perky agent. She was a real twinkie. Her name tag told me her name was Sandy. We will soon be a nation of no last names, I think.

"Good morning. My name is Sudduth Spencer. This is Miss Baby Soniat. A funny thing happened to us on the way to Norfolk.

" ...So you see. I'll give you her jewelry as well as my father's wristwatch and both my class and signet rings. The watch is twenty-two karat gold. No, ah...Sandy, not the band, just the watch. The original band was alligator, but I

197

prefer grosgrain straps. You give them to the captain as collateral. When we reach New Orleans, I'll go to my apartment and return with the money. Now, Miss Soniat's two rings alone are worth ... how much, Baby?"

"At the time of Aunt Valkyrie's death the rings were appraised for $19,300. But that was several years ago, Suddie. Why I should think Miss ... honey, don't you have a last name? I just hate calli...."

"Thank you, Baby, that's all we need to know. Well, Sandy, what will it be? Yes or no?"

"Sir, this is highly irregular." She was pretty, but not bright.

"So was last night," I snapped.

"Let me speak to my supervisor," she said before disappearing.

"You need a shave, Suddie, your hair is sticking straight up in the back and your breath reeks," Baby cranked.

"Darlin', I admit it's a great pity that one is never good-looking when one wants most to be," I said, somewhat nettled and thin lipped.

"What do you mean by that, Sudduth?" Baby asked indignantly.

"Nothing, honey, I'm teasing. That's all. You're always beautiful. To me, especially."

"I think I'm catching a cold," Baby said without so much as a thank you very much.

"You're such a child, Baby. Here. I'll give you back my jacket 'til we board. Then I'll get you a blanket."

When Sandy finally returned, she had her supervisor with her.

"You've had quite an adventure, Mr. Spencer. We'll let you board, and you can keep your possessions. However, we'll keep Miss Soniat at the terminal until you return. I've arranged for someone to drive you to your car."

" 'Thank' you seems inadequate. But I... we thank you both very much."

Sandy flashed me a brilliant smile and said:

"Thank you for flying Delta. How many bags will you be checking?"

Well, Leeds Weber was dead now. So what. He was an asshole to the end. That's when I decided to go to the St. Thomas Housing Project down by the river. I had no wish to end up an asshole, and if I did it myself my insurance wouldn't pay Mother anything. It was during Carnival. Mayday Martinay and I were leaving a queen's breakfast at the Roosevelt, which began as the Gruenwald and is now called the Fairmont. I was cabbing it since my driver's license had been revoked for sixty days. At Mayday's, I declined her kind offer for a nightcap and returned to the waiting cab. As the driver turned on to Magazine, I told him I felt like walking.

"You feel like walking at three in the morning?" he asked, turning around to stare at me open-mouthed.

"That's right. Stop here, please," I answered.

"You Uptown people are nuts. You know that?"

"I know that. Keep the change. Good night or good morning, whatever."

"You OK, Mister?"

"I'm fine, thank you," I replied as I shut the door.

I walked the rest of the way. It must have been a slow night. Surely not everyone was asleep. The St. Thomas Housing Project is located in what is known as the Irish Channel. It is the area between Constance Street and the river extending from St. Joseph Street to Louisiana Avenue. Almost from the time of sailors coming into port, ones who watched for a light kept burning in an all-night saloon, the district has been known as one of the city's rougher spots. Many Irish died digging the canals of New Orleans. Employers preferred them to slaves because they entailed no legal responsibility and when they died there were always others waiting for their jobs. Sad but true. After a while I sat down on a graffiti-covered bench to have another cigarette. I was thinking that this might be my last one when I heard steps and then this voice speaking to me. At last. I hoped it would be fast. I don't like pain.

"You lost, Mister?"

"No, I'm not lost."

"What you doing here, Mister?"

"I'm having a cigarette."

"You ought not be here. You belong Uptown."

He stepped out of the shadows and sat down next to me. He was a child.

"That may be," I say, "but you should be in bed. How old are you? Thirteen? Fourteen?"

"If I should be in bed, so should you. You'll

get yourself killed down here. Even if you wasn't dressed so fine."

"That's the general idea, son."

"You don't know what you're talking about, Mister. What you want to die for? Hell, I could live to be a hundred and never be dressed so fine or go to balls, because I know that's where you been. Man, you think about that while I hot-wire my mama's car and drive you home. If you don't let me, I'll go in the house and call the police. They'd be here like that. They'd put you in the crazy place for sure. What you say? What you gonna do?"

What's it all about, Alfie? I contemplated.

I recalled something Rayne had jeered at me about. Something to do with my only being liked by princes or paupers and not really knowing anyone in between.

To which I had replied:

"Papa always maintained that manners are manners. Whether one be a prince or a pauper."

"Jesus," she had spat.

"I think it's time to go home, son. Thank you."

My breakdown culminated, as did my ascent from a dungeon deep, at yet another Queen's Breakfast. I was so drunk I fell while dancing with Nefertiti Bethell and badly broke my nose. Being drunk and bleeding in white tie and tails is totally different from being drunk and bleeding in khaki trousers and a blue oxford cloth shirt. There was also the matter of the smashed face of my great-great-grandfather's heavy gold pocket watch that had made it through the War.

When I called Nefertiti to apologize, the thoroughbred that she is replied:

"Suddie, darlin', don't give it the time of day. Daddy did it all the time, and so does Niles for that matter."

Nefertiti's father, Carnarvon Bethell, had shot himself through the head in his wife's dressing room shortly after his mistress, Havana Owen's, neck was broken. Some degenerate hippie, stoned on marijuana, fell out of a tree as she rode Thebes, her chestnut mare, in Audubon Park. The horse had been Carnarvon's birthday present to her the year before.

Havana Owen, besides having the city's most beautiful neck, had the city's largest collection of Biedermeier furniture. Her late husband had indulged her passion for blonde, monumental, and architectonic furniture, and Carnarvon had satisfied it even more while satisfying his.

There has always been a natural affinity between us, the Uptowners, and Egypt. We were both great river dynasties. They had King Tutankhamen. We had King Cotton. Each of us worship river nymphs. That's the sisterhood of minor river deities who dwell in bodies of water and have the power to possess the minds and bodies of men and fill them with demonic enthusiasm and excessive sexual desire. To eat of this lotus is to be under their spell forever.

All this natural affinity reached epic proportions of religious-experience fervor when the King Tut exhibit opened at Delgado Museum in 1977. People mobbed City Park for months. Some had visions. Others just renamed their dogs.

This natural affinity resulted in the New Leviathan Oriental Foxtrot Orchestra's issuing their famous album entitled "Old King Tut: A Voyage Down The River Nile, Commemorating The New Orleans Museum of Arts 1977 Exhibition for Eye: Egyptian Images and Inscriptions." What the hell all this means I have no idea. But the record is a classic that features such ageless songs as "Belles of Baghdad," "Under The Mellow Arabian Moon," and the not-to-be-believed, but sublimely tuneful, "If You Sheik On Your Mama, Your Mama's Gonna Sheba On You."

I was in the coffee shop at the "Ponch" having a slice of Mile-High pie when everybody's favorite waitress, Darlene, told me she didn't think King Tut was so grand.

"Really?" I asked.

"That's right, Mr. Spencer."

"Well, why, Darlene?"

"Shoot, everybody knows that all the best or important people stays at the "Ponch," and if he's so important why he staying out at City Park?"

"You have a point, Darlene."

Even though the Bethells are Egyptian crazy, Nefertiti's choice of words hurt, considering the

203

sad state of Major Dabney Ball's, late of Fifth Virginia Cavalry, pocketwatch. There was no way I could tell the time of day on the watch of this brave gentleman-soldier-ancestor who had lost his right arm in the Battle of Antietam and continued to fight. In fact, Major General J.E.B. Stuart's letter to him is now in the National Archives in Washington, D.C.

The saga of this watch is so far-fetched as to be grotesque. The Uptown jeweler, Adler's, which is located downtown on Canal Street, "sadly informed" me that the watch was a "lost cause," too. Distressed didn't even begin to describe how I felt, especially when other jewelers concurred. I had just about given up all hope when I discovered, by chance, a small shop on Chartres Street not far from the house built for Napoleon. It is now a bar of a certain musty, decadent allure and known by the cognoscenti as the place to go when in need of a muffaletta, that large roll of pleasure bulging with ham and olive salad, mortadella sausage, provolone cheese, Genoa salami, olive oil, and sesame seeds. It was also here that Rayne, she of the caustic flicks, who loved the Quarter, in one of her moments of tenderness for me fed me brie on buttered French bread as some opera blared forth from scratched records played on a gramophone. From a house fit for an Emperor to a bar: sic transit gloria mundi. This should tell you something.

Anyway, this very old German jeweler, who was actually a silversmith, owned the nearby shop. He told me about this olympian watch and clockmaker operating out of his house in the Faubourg Marigny section.

So I called this master horologist to arrange a time and to get directions. I was cross and in a bad mood. My nose also hurt like hell. But I knew I could rise to the occasion. I drove to this depressing neighborhood of local artisans and workmen, parked, and knocked on the door of a house that shouted for paint.

"It's open," a voice yelled out.

I opened the door into what was once a living room. There must have been about two hundred clocks ticking away. All that ticking started to give me a headache.

"How do you do," I said. "I'm Sudduth Spencer. This is the pocketwatch we discussed."

I handed the watch to a man in a wheelchair. He had no legs. He said nothing. He just stared at me.

He took the watch and began to carefully examine my smashed treasure. Nothing was said and the clocks were driving me crazy.

"This is a very valuable timepiece, Mr. Spencer. I never handled one of this quality. It would be a joy to work on," he said looking up at me at last.

"Then it can be repaired. That's splendid. Super. Thank you. What a relief. I was told you were a champion."

"Oh, yes, Mr. Spencer, I could put it back in shape, but I won't."

"I don't understand. You have the ability to repair my watch and you won't?" I was incredulous.

"That's right, Mr. Spencer."

"Why not?" I asked.

"Because I know how this watch came to be smashed."

"That's impossible," I shot back.

"No, it isn't. My son is a waiter at the country club on weekends. He told me about this fine man who was dead drunk, too drunk to be doing the Charleston. You slipped while dancing and smashed your nose, smashed this watch, and bled all over yourself, as well as over your woman's expensive dress. Then you got up and fell on a waiter carrying a tray of dishes. Dishes he ended up having to pay for. Your being drunk cost him half his wages. To your credit, however, the boy said you were a perfect gentleman. Apologized. Said you were sorry."

I pulled out some money. "Will this cover the cost of.... "

"I don't want your money, Mr. Spencer, nor does he, but it's decent of you. Verifies how my son felt about you. Now, what in the hell reason you have for being drunk, I don't care about. You Uptown people are always having breakdowns. All that privilege and you have breakdowns. Well, I have ability and I won't repair your watch."

"You're a very harsh judge," I replied. It was all I could say.

"Perhaps I am, but that's my privilege."

So I finally stopped drinking, but I could not forget or replace Baby. I only drank to kill the knot in the pit of my stomach, anyway. Never to forget her.

Oliver died of cirrhosis of the liver the following year. In death, as in life, Oliver was kind
to me. I was not forgotten. Oliver left me ten
thousand dollars. Carrebee's was sold. On my
last day, Oliver, Jr. walked in my office and handed
me the ornate brass safe dial that he had had
removed from the wall safe in Bookkeeping.

"Thought you might like this," he said, and
smiled for the first time, ever.

Perhaps we could have become friends?

I had no wish to move to Chicago. When I
was offered a position in Washington, D.C. I
accepted. Washington was at least Southern and
I had relatives and friends there. I could never
live where I was unconnected and rootless.

On that last Friday morning I was going
to Carrebee's to finish going through my now
beloved rolltop desk. Saturday morning, I was
leaving on a jet plane. Alone at the streetcar
stop near Mother's house, I felt the way one
feels on the morning one suddenly realizes
one's clothing no longer has name tags sewn
inside them. Only the snapping of the streetcar's
doors opening made me aware of its arrival. I
looked up and there he was, unchanged. My
friend, the black streetcar conductor. I jumped
on.

"Where in the world have you been?" I asked.
"I've been worried sick about you. I thought you
died or were killed. I even called the transit
company. Spoke to the head of personnel." To
hell with those listening. I didn't care. He was
my friend.

What was he saying?

"Why are you whispering? Do you have laryngitis?"

I bent down.

"I can't hear you."

"I said, I was reported for being uppity the day of the big ice. They put me on the dead man's shift. Midnight to seven in the morning. I sure have missed you."

"Well, I've missed you, too. I sure have. I'm so happy and relieved to see you again."

He smiled. "You still looking fine. Best looking white man I ever saw. Just seeing you makes me feel good deep inside. Come Monday, it will be just the same with us. Right? Same in the evening, too? Right?"

"Afraid not," I replied.

"Why? What you mean? You made a new black friend?" He sounded so hurt.

"No. Of course not. But, I'm leaving tomorrow for Washington, D.C. on the big bird Delta. To a new job."

"But you have a fine job here."

"Not anymore. The company was sold. As of this morning, I have no job at all."

"You're bound for glory and you'll forget me," he said sadly.

"I doubt that. My days of glory are over, but I'll have a job. I won't forget you. I couldn't."

"Promise?"

"I promise."

"Not ever?"

"Not ever."

"Well, I guess you best be getting off."

"Why?"

Good Lord, we had talked all the way to Carrebee's.

"Goodbye," I said. "Take care of yourself."

We shook hands.

I stepped off and turned to wave. He waved and the doors slammed shut. He waited 'til I had crossed the street, then he clanked the bell, lowered his side window, and yelled out:

"Bound for glory, yes you are!"

I waved. I waved again. I never saw him again and I never knew his name.

* * *

13

The city was in a white heat the morning I returned to New Orleans for a bittersweet celebration of Mack's life. A celebration she would have dearly loved because in our great Southern Babylon we know how to balance disaster with joy. That's why there are so many benevolent societies and burial clubs in New Orleans. And basic in every burial contract is the provision for a jazz funeral. Why, the city coroner plays in the Olympia Brass Jazz Band.

"A man or woman who couldn't make themselves sure of a fine burial—God, what a shame!" Mack had lamented time and time again.

Mack's interest in "anybody's" funeral was exceeded only by my grandmother's life-long fascination with death. Each woman could converse for hours over the smallest details and nuances of their most recent funeral. Nana especially favored Irish and Italian funerals. They were the most "majestic" with their grief.

"Oh, Mack, you really should have been there. Eight women besides the widow threw themselves on the casket, and one poor soul actually had to be stopped from climbing into the coffin. Now this was a man who was beloved."

"Lord, but you are lucky, Miss Eva E," Mack would say. "Only six people fainted at the service I attended yesterday and the flowers were real puny, but the wailing was something terrible and the best I've heard in, I know, three months."

The noted undertaker, Dr. Ambrose Funteroy, was held in very high regard by Mack. Dr. Funteroy permitted her to sit on a stool and watch as he embalmed and beautified a person. Nana would listen with the greatest interest when Mack told her all she had seen, but always declined to accompany her mainly because she believed an unclothed body was indecent. I can still see Nana coming through the front door and handing hat, gloves, and bag to Daniel and all the while exclaiming:

"Really, it was the best funeral I ever attended."

We remember our dead too, keep them in mind, visit them, leave flowers for them and observe the occasion of supreme remembrance, All Saints' Day, every November first, by thronging to cemeteries to place flowers on graves with a fervor that almost rivals that of Mardi Gras.

How many times had Nana and I picnicked at Metairie Cemetery surrounded by the grandeur of November chrysanthemums and above-ground tombs so crowded together in spots that only a few inches of space intervenes between them? Picnicked on such taken-for-granted delicacies as cheese straws tangy with cayenne pepper, beaten biscuits no larger than a quarter filled with paper-thin slivers of ham from the heart of the shank, and equally thin slices of cucumbers on buttered circles of white and whole wheat bread—and best of all, two wedges of Lady Baltimore Cake.

Many visitors think of our cemeteries as cities of the dead. In a way, I guess they do look like miniature cities, complete with little streets and fences around the "elaborate buildings." Metairie Cemetery, the largest and most elaborate in a city of many, became a cemetery when the Metairie Jockey Club and race course closed in 1872.

"Always remember who you are Sudduth," Nana told me on one of the last times I went to Metairie with her. "It will console you in bad times. I've outlived the sixteen men who loved me and I only loved one."

"The Senator," I interrupted.

"No, child, not the Senator."

"Not the Senator, Nana?" I wanted to cry.

"Don't cry, Sudduth, the Senator never knew. Your mother knew. She heard me talking to Mack. Now you know and, of course, I always knew."

"Who was he, Nana?"

"A gentleman never asks personal or embarrassing questions, Sudduth. You surprise me. But I shall tell you why I didn't marry him. He was married and he was killed. If he hadn't died, well. . . ."

"Are you sure the Senator never knew?" I had to know.

"One is only sure about dying, Sudduth. If the Senator knew, he kept it to himself. He was a gentleman, Sudduth. You are a gentleman. If you were poor, you would still be a gentleman. Money does not make a gentleman. Who you are and who you were makes a gentleman. Don't abuse it and always be kind to others. Remember it is God, Grace, and Grandfather. Not you. You may kiss me now if you like, Sudduth."

"I like. I always like, Nana."

Mack died at ninety-three. Blind. Mother had nursed her the last months of her life. Now she was going out in even more style than she had provided for.

Baby was waiting outside the Gethsemane Temple Church on Duffosat Street.

"Morning, Arabella. Morning, Sudduth," she said.

"How sweet of you to come, Baby," Mother said, kissing her. "I must go see to things, but come sit with us."

"Your mama said you were flying down. She's taking it badly, isn't she?"

"Yes, she . . . we loved Mack very much. Mama will be all alone now. They understood each other, you know."

"How long shall you be at your mama's?" she asked.

"Not long, Baby."

"How long is not long?"

"Baby, I see no. . . . "

"How long, damnit?"

"I'm flying back Saturday morning."

"I'll drive you to the airport. What time is your flight?"

"That won't be necessary."

"Suddie, I'm trying. . . . "

"Trying to what?"

"Trying to say I'm sorry and you won't even talk to me."

"There's nothing left to say, Baby. We stopped talking over five years ago, the night of Pierrot's party, as I recall, and I haven't forgotten our conversation. I'd best be going in. Thank you for coming. Mack would have liked it."

Baby's famous neck was finally beginning to go. Her gloved hand kept fiddling with the piece of gossamerly exquisite silk at her throat. But she was still beautiful, at least to me. Had anyone ever worn clothes better? I thought. Even for a funeral, she was still the Double Queen.

I recalled her "two drawers full of fraternity pins that I'll have melted down for a gold neck-band when this aristocratic neck goes."

Involuntarily knowing what had flashed across my mind, she pulled the silk away and, looking at me with eyes that were now Stebo's, raised her chin.

A thoroughbred to the core, I thought. If nothing else, she would not have pity. Mine or anyone's.

"I'm staying," she said.

"Suit yourself," I replied.

Baby stood in the back of the church that was too small to accommodate all of the people

Mack knew, black and white. Considering the en masse turnout of what was left of the ancien régime, Mack had at one time or another nannied many an Uptown baby. Even Judge Raoul Hampton and Miss Blanche were in attendance. I had not seen them since the ill-fated 1812 Ball. The Hampton boys, twins I remembered being told, had died young. I thought how the times that bred Mack, the Hamptons, and us were as dead as Mack.

Electric fans droned without end and merged with the Reverend Earl Jupiter's dull humming voice boring through my brain. I felt sick from the closeness of the church and overwhelmed by the scent from masses of floral tributes. Mack was in that coffin in front of the altar, but all I could think about was how tired I was, more tired than I had ever been in all my life. I was exhausted in body and drained of emotions. I would think about Mack later. I had the rest of my life to think of Papa, the Senator, Nana, Frances, Daniel, Mack, and Baby. Yes, I had the rest of my life to think and remember.

"I am the resurrection and the life, sayeth the Lord; He that believeth in me, though he were dead, yet shall he live; and whosoever believeth in me shall never die." The service was finally over. The Reverend Earl Jupiter finally stopped preaching.

On the way to St. Peter's Cemetery on Valence Street the members of the Olympia Brass Jazz Band walked reposefully. A few steps—halt. A few more steps—long pause. Matched-plumed horses pulled the hearse. The prolonged, dirge-

216

like moaning was overpowering in its emotional compulsion. Not much longer, not much longer, I thought. We marched in slow and mournful cadence behind them until the hearse entered the cemetery and the soul was "freed" at the grave site. Over. Over at last. The flower-decorated umbrellas opened. The tempo changed. The band switched to "When The Saints Go Marchin' In" and dancing broke out in full swing. Mother's small white hand kept disappearing. There were so many hands to shake. "The Mahogany Hall Stomp" was making everybody happy.

Baby hugged Mother and walked over to where Jackie Bolton and I were talking. Baby stood there looking at me. Walter died my second year in Washington. Jackie misses him terribly. They were wonderful together. Always gay. Always laughing. Always happy. Baby just stood there waiting. Waiting. Jackie kept looking over at her, but continued on.

"I just may visit Washington, Sudduth. Perhaps after France."

I said, "Fine. Shall look forward to seeing you."

I kissed Jackie goodbye and turned to Baby. "All right, we'll talk."

The sun was at its zenith, as we walked to a patriarchal oak to escape its rays and our shadows. The tree reminded me of the Suicide Oak out in City Park, not far from the Delgado Museum of Art. Here, under the oak's enveloping branches, disconsolate lovers and bankrupts of all kinds committed suicide. Shit. What a city, I thought. A suicide oak, and not far away, the

217

Dueling Oaks where affairs of honor were settled by sword or pistol and afterwards coffee for one.

Sheltered by the tree's shade we stood there, mute, the fragments of our lives about us. At the end of the procession, the band was playing the "Basin Street Blues."

"Suddie, I've said I'm sorry," Baby began. "What more do you want?"

"I never wanted 'I'm sorry,' that's for damn sure. I wanted 'I love you.' I wanted you to love me the way you love Stebo. But it doesn't matter now. And sorry doesn't assuage what we did to each other."

"You're different, Suddie. You've changed," was all she said.

"Have I?" I answered.

"Yes, you have. What changed you?" she asked.

"Let's just say it's harder to avoid the unattractive parts of life."

"Well, I haven't changed. Have I?" she asked somewhat coquettishly.

"No, Baby, you're still a child. My childless Childe. Only a child could think 'I'm sorry' makes up for so many hurts."

But she had changed. That deathless vitality that made all other women appear less had faded away as imperceptibly as the quantity and quality of orange peel have been diminished in marmalade. That special sweetness and way of looking at a man had been replaced by divine right and her empire was now the ever-changing faces of deprived grammar school students.

"You're not going to forgive me?" she asked.

"No," I replied.

But hadn't I promised to always love her? she rejoined.

That had been my second mistake, I said and turned to walk back. I kept walking. I, who once could have denied her nothing, kept walking. I did not tell her my first mistake had been to love an illusion. I was worn out from loving and forgiving an illusion. The band was playing "Do You Know What It Means To Miss New Orleans."

Do you know what it means to miss New Orleans? I saw the Roman Candy Man coming up Valence Street. Yes, I know what it means to miss New Orleans. Where else would the grandson of the horse-drawn wagon's original owner, who began selling on the streets of Uptown in 1915, still make Roman Chewing Candy by the old recipe on a little burner in the wagon and still only charge fifteen cents a stick.

People were leaving. I nodded to them, waved to others, and smiled. I walked up to Mama and put my hand on her shoulder.

"Let's go home, Mama. You're tired."

"Yes, Raiford, darlin', I'm tired. Do take me home, please."

What's it all about, Alfie? Who knows? Perhaps it's about the Broadwater Beach Hotel and Baby, in white linen, seated on a marble-topped walnut bar eating maraschino cherries from an iced bowl. Or it's about how she had glowed with affecting charm and, how, at her best, she was always irresistible. Or, even about how the very best of me had belonged to her, and about the melancholy woven into my joie de vivre because of the wear and tear of proximity and ruinous romanticism. Whatever, she is forever lanterns and fireflies and days that swim in a haze of sunshine and ease. And, to her credit, she had never been humdrum. None of us had ever been humdrum. Even now, I cannot tolerate humdrum. And, God knows, the world has become humdrum. Think about it. Today's world is boring itself to death. The talking classes are doing it to us. Don't they know reformers are always forgotten? It's the memoirs of the frivolous that are always read.

Shakespeare not withstanding, our fortunes may indeed lie in our stars, and not in ourselves. Until now, my life has been something I never questioned. I simply accepted it. I am the person I am because heredity and environment prevented my being anything else. I am a Southerner. I was born into a world of beauty, grace, and style, and will die amid ugliness. I have outlived my era, loathe the present, and, harboring no guilt for having lived off the cream at the top of a bottle of milk, am too fastidious for an homogenized future.

I will always believe that water rises to its own level, that original nastiness is worse than original sin, and progress nothing but disintegration. Baby had ensorcelled me for over twenty-five years, and the substitute for her had been a chain of flirtations with a woman for every link. It was said I never had an affair that lasted longer than the asparagus season. It was true. Except for Baby, my affairs were conducted on the level of a civilized uncommitted exchange of pleasure with its national anthem being "Just One of Those Things." Now they are conducted only to prove that I can still have asparagus on my plate. Only with Baby had I experienced the agonies, ecstasies, and uncertainties of love.

For a lifetime I had only been half a person and Baby the other half. She had been my religion. My private paganism. I don't damn Baby for burning out and quieting down. I don't damn her for ceasing to stir up life. I do damn her for reaching the end of the Primrose Path still selfish, with character no deeper than a penny. I damn myself most of all for no longer wanting her.

When she became world-weary, I became old. With youth gone, I am left with neither pleasure nor pain. But pain is not far off. I am graying and slower. Although my blithe spirit has been lost, my ingrained love for that luxuriously assured life remains. The bright day is done and we are for the dark. I want yesterday. I need God.

* * *

To those who
have been uniformly kind
in giving encouragement, I thank
Cam Miller; Mary Ann Ferguson; Dr. Roger Easson;
Fielding Marshall; Sandra Plant; Eileen Hiler, whose
love for my "characters" inspired the painting
"Jackson Square"; and Phyllis Tickle, publisher,
editor and now friend.